CUSTOMER SERVICE EXCELLENCE

Libraries & Archives

00884\DTP\RN\07.07   LIB 7

GUNS ACROSS RED RIVER

GUNS ACROSS RED RIVER

by

Hugh Martin

Dales Large Print Books
Long Preston, North Yorkshire,
BD23 4ND, England.

British Library Cataloguing in Publication Data.

Martin, Hugh
    Guns across Red River.

    A catalogue record of this book is
    available from the British Library

    ISBN   978-1-84262-619-1 pbk

First published in Great Britain 2006 by Robert Hale Limited

Published in Large Print 2008 by arrangement with
Robert Hale Ltd.

Dales Large Print is an imprint of Library Magna Books Ltd.

Printed and bound in Great Britain by
T.J. (International) Ltd., Cornwall, PL28 8RW

For my sister, Frances,
and four more:
Roberta Scott and Jerry Pippin
in Muskogee in the old Indian Territory
and Ken and Jill Taylor in Essex

CHAPTER ONE

DANNEHAR COMES – AND GOES!

The brand of the gunfighter was burned good and bold on Cephas Dannehar. One could hardly miss it, of course, in the big Peacemaker Colt, worn low and tied down to the right leg of his faded jeans. Then there was the whole persona of the man, his way of moving as if constantly on the watch and his garb, close to that of a working cowhand, but not quite geared to the practicalities of chasing beef on the hoof. The face under the brim of the black sombrero was seamed and weather-punished and no longer young but the dark eyes were bright and alert with the same hair-trigger watchfulness which infused his movements.

Slim Oskin, marshal of Cinch City, halted briefly just as he turned a corner into Main Street and took in the sight of Dannehar swinging easily down from the saddle of his black bronc outside the modest structure of McNiff's Hotel.

'Well, I'll be damned!' he growled. 'As if things weren't bad enough, now I've got Cephas Dannehar to contend with!'

The lawman, tall and rangy and carrying years which closely totalled Dannehar's, set off up the boardwalk in the newcomer's direction, hugging the clapboard buildings, attempting to ensure that he reached Dannehar before he was spotted. Since Dannehar had his back to him and was occupied in securing his rein to the hitch-rack, his usual caution was thwarted and the lawman was wholly successful.

Cephas Dannehar felt the marshal's sixgun prod into his back and stay there.

'Hello, Cephas. Can it be you're growing old, letting a man get the drop on you? Reach up and don't think of grabbing your iron,' he growled.

'Well, by cracky! Slim Oskin! I'd know that unmusical voice anywhere,' responded Dannehar in an unruffled way as he obeyed the law officer. 'I passed your office and gaol back yonder and was plumb surprised to see that fancy sign: "James J Oskin, Town Marshal". It was pleasant to think I had an old friend in a strange town and was looking forward to meeting you – but not like this. What ails you, Slim? I'm not on the dodge –

there's no reward out for me.'

'It's town policy, Cephas. The council passed an ordinance requiring all strangers carrying guns to be held for twenty-four hours until they're checked out. It's all due to the kind of undesirable ranahans who've all too often passed through town and made themselves objectionable while here. Mostly, they've been on the way into the Nations to cause trouble. Now, turn around slowly and keep your hands up.'

Dannehar complied, objecting, 'You can't do that, Slim. What about *habeas corpus?*'

Oskin laughed. 'You've been a lawman in your time, Cephas, and you know a suspect can be held for twenty-four hours without any writ of *habeas corpus* being needed. Anyway, this is Texas and we have been known to make the law by rule of thumb. But not in this case. The council requires me to make a record of those arriving in town openly bearing arms and I'm paid to follow orders. Cinch City they call this place, because it sits on the border with Indian Territory like the buckle on a cinch strap and we aim to keep it tight like a cinch – tight, peaceful and respectable.'

From the corner of his eye, Dannehar was aware of a third party cautiously making a sidewise approach to the marshal and himself. He halted beside Oskin and revealed himself as a slim young man, wearing a deputy's star and levelling a sixshooter.

Oskin nodded towards the young man. 'This here's Dick Meader, my deputy, as smart a young fellow as you could have at your side, even if he is a bit impetuous. But then, we were, too, when we were his age, weren't we?' Then, to Meader: 'Put up your gun, Dick. Mr Dannehar doesn't need more than one weapon pointing at him. He's a reasonable man by and large.'

'Dannehar!' gasped the deputy. 'You mean this is *Cephas* Dannehar? Why, I've heard about him and his doings long ago in Dodge City, El Paso and Lordsburg.'

Dannehar grinned and said, 'You might mention Tombstone, Carson City and Deadwood while you're at it. Marshal Oskin here was in on some of those capers with me but you don't have to stress how long ago it was. Old as we are, neither one of us is a museum piece yet.'

'No, but old enough to appreciate the benefits of a quieter and more settled life – at least one of us is,' put in Oskin.

'So, now you do exactly as the town council orders, like holding me at gunpoint, fixing to lodge me in your gaol,' complained Dannehar. 'Dammit, Slim, I have things to see to. All I aimed to do here was get a bite to eat at the hotel then be on my way.'

'No hard feelings, Cephas,' Oskin replied. 'I'll get Horace McNiff at the hotel to fix you one of his best meals and bring it over to the gaol. I'll see that your horse is settled at the livery stable yonder, watered and fed, but I'll hold you and your gun for twenty-four hours because you rode into town openly bearing arms. Fact is, Cinch City aims to be in the forefront of the drive for law and order. Even you must admit that times are changing and the old days are rapidly disappearing over the hill.'

'Well, it's a hell of a way to treat an old partner,' growled Dannehar.

'Just a matter of precaution, Cephas,' responded Oskin. 'There's all too many trigger-happy roughnecks, liquor pedlars and those who'd steal the land from the Indians sneaking into Indian Territory. It ain't my duty to stop 'em crossing the line but a night in gaol before they move on prevents any hell-raising in my town. After a taste of Cinch City's hospitality, they're plumb anxious to move on when I kick 'em out of the hoosegow in the morning. So just

13

allow Dick to unbuckle your gun-gear, then you can lower your arms. And think how, in years to come, Dick can boast to his grandkids that he relieved the great Cephas Dannehar of his gun.'

Divested of his Peacemaker and gun-belt by the young deputy, Dannehar was marched across the street towards the jail and, though Slim Oskin still levelled a naked sixgun, he did not make it too obvious that the newcomer was under arrest. Maintaining his bantering friendliness, the lawman asked, 'What're you doing in this country, anyway, Cephas? Don't tell me you, too, are headed for the Indian Nations for no good purpose.'

'I'm bound for the Nations all right, Slim,' said the prisoner. 'As I told you, I have appointments to keep but the nature of my business is my own affair. You disappoint me, though, if you think there might be no good purpose in it.'

'Well, I can think of a few things you were involved in that weren't any too saintly,' said Oskin.

'And *I* can recall the fellow who partnered me in some of 'em – a fellow I don't have to go too far to find at this very moment,' countered Dannehar. 'Those were the great days, when we were young and full of fire.'

14

He gave a sigh which sounded almost nostalgic.

'Well, I was plumb full of stupidity, too,' grunted the lawman as they stepped into the warped wooden structure of the gaol. 'Never did fully understand why I hooked up with you, anyhow. If ever a man was ornery and mule-headed, it was you.'

Young Deputy Dick Meader listened fascinatedly to this exchange. It was plain to him that between Town Marshal Slim Oskin and the old frontier gunhand he had arrested there was an enduring friendship, doubtless born on the wild trails of long ago. The strange thing was that, though he complained, Cephas Dannehar seemed to fully understand Oskin's present position. His objections had a bantering quality which denoted that he did not consider the lawman to be treacherous. Quite likely, he privately acknowledged that he was a forceful and efficient peace officer.

'Yes, you were always mule-headed, Cephas,' continued Oskin. 'Always making the wrong choice, like fighting on the wrong side in the big war for instance.'

'I might have been on the side that lost,' said Dannehar spiritedly, 'but I don't for a minute regret doing my best in the company

15

of brave men.'

'Well, I'll give you that,' murmured Oskin on a note of penitence. 'There were plenty of brave men on your side and mine, blue or grey, and there was too much suffering, whatever the colour of a man's pants, and too many widows and orphans resulting. How do you like my gaol?'

Dannehar looked around. 'It ain't much,' he commented. 'It's too cramped. Sheriff Slaughter's place back in Tombstone in the old days was better than this and the Lord knows that was bad enough.' The gaol was indeed cramped. It had a single passageway running straight though the clapboard building from the street. On one side there was a single doorway, open and revealing the marshal's office. Opposite this was the large, barred gate of a single cell. Inside the cell, sitting on a bench, was a young man in range gear. He was bearded with several days' growth and looked distinctly un-savoury. He watched the approach of the two lawmen and the prisoner with dark, distrustful eyes.

'I forgot to mention that you'll have a companion in the guest room,' said Oskin. 'He says his name is Cal Stebbins. He came in a couple of hours ago sporting a Navy

16

Colt at his belt, so he's getting the same treatment as you. You can look him over and make your own judgement of him.'

Dannehar did and didn't like what he saw. The kid looked as though he thought he was tough and, quite likely, he was the kind of drifter upon which Oskin was keeping a keen eye: the dangerous sort who were attracted to Indian Territory with its rocky law-structure and its opportunities for illegal money-making and deviltry.

Deputy Dick Meader took a large key from a nail on the wall and opened the cell. Dannehar entered voluntarily and the set of bars clanged behind him.

'This is a memorable moment for you, Mr Stebbins,' Oskin told the glowering youth already occupying the cell. 'Now you can write in your memoirs how you had the honour of sharing quarters with the dis-tinguished Cephas Dannehar – assuming you can write, that is.'

The youth in the cell responded with a curl of his unshaven lip.

The two lawmen retreated to the office opposite the cell to deposit Dannehar's gun-gear, then Slim Oskin emerged and said through the cell bars, 'Dick will bring you some of McNiff's best grub from the hotel shortly, Cephas.'

'Best grub from the hotel!' echoed Dannehar's cell-mate. 'Don't I get the same?'

'No, you don't because *you* ain't the distinguished Cephas Dannehar,' responded Oskin. 'You get bread, meat and coffee, and even that is too good for you.'

The lawman turned on his heel and headed towards the street door. 'I'm taking a turn around the town. Dick is in the office. In due course, he'll feed you. I'd advise you to settle down and make the best of it', he announced. Then he walked into the sunlit street.

Dannehar and the youth sized each other up. Dannehar saw a stringy kid in the greasy and worn gear of a cowhand and with a battered black sombrero. His foxy, unshaven face made itself no more attractive or trustworthy on closer inspection than when Dannehar first glimpsed it. The kid saw a rangy, ageing man with hardly a pick of spare flesh on him and there was clearly plenty of spring in his spare frame. His face was hawkish, lined by the suns and winds of many seasons and the dark eyes under his shaggy brows were bright and alert, seemingly undimmed by the passage of time. Those of more mature judgement might have seen signs in this man which gave warning of the need for caution in his company, but the kid was not of mature judgement. He was unimpressed and he said so.

'The distinguished Cephas Dannehar!' he scorned with the curl of his lip which seemed to be his trademark. 'The pistoleer from way back who could hold up a town or tame it as the mood took him yet he gets himself nabbed by hick lawmen in a hick town and lands himself in gaol.'

Dannehar's face creased slowly into a knowing grin. 'I wouldn't be so fast to call Marshal Oskin a hick if I was you, son,' he said. 'I'll warrant he nabbed you without too much trouble. As for how distinguished Cephas Dannehar is, just stick around and you might learn a thing or two.'

'I ain't got no choice but to stick around,' grumbled Cal Stebbins.

'Nor me,' drawled Dannehar lazily. 'So, I aim to rest up a spell.' As if showing total disdain for his cellmate, he lay himself full length on the bench opposite the one occupied by Stebbins, took off his hat, planted it on his chest and closed his eyes.

After ten minutes or so of what looked like drowsy repose, Dannehar said, without opening his eyes, 'How do they dish up the grub here?'

'Huh!' grunted his cellmate. 'We're cooped up in this darned hoosegow and, you, claiming to teach me a thing or two, can only think about grub.'

'Sure thing,' answered Dannehar. 'After all, I'm due for some special treatment – good grub from the hotel – too bad you can't look forward to the same. I might as well enjoy it while I'm here. Now, how's the grub served here? I mean who brings it in?'

'The deputy brings it right into the cell on a tray and the marshal stands in the passage with his gun drawn while we eat.'

'That's what I figured,' said Dannehar drowsily. 'There's no hatchway in that barred gate to allow grub to be passed in. Then I suppose the deputy waits here in the cell until we finish and he takes out the empty plates and cups while, all the time, the marshal keeps us covered from outside until the gate is locked again?'

'Sure, that's how it's done.'

Still with his eyes closed, Dannehar stipulated in a low tone, 'Now listen, kid, and don't louse this up. When the deputy brings in the grub, we eat it in the ordinary way and when he collects the plates on his tray, you stand near him with your hat in

20

your hand. I'll be standing close to him, too. Just as he makes for the door, burdened with the tray, you quickly shove your hat into his face – you bury his face inside the hat, understand? Shove him backward, right off his feet if you can.'

'What? And have the marshal shoot me from the passage?' objected Stebbins.

'He won't get the chance,' grunted Dannehar. 'I'll take care of him because, as you go into the hat trick, I'll snatch the deputy's gun from his holster...'

'...and you shoot the marshal!' concluded Stebbins with relish.

'Just leave all that to me,' emphasized Dannehar. 'You dash out across the passage to the office, find our guns and bring 'em out quick.'

'Then what?' asked the youngster.

'Then we take off across the street to the livery stable for our cayuses and hightail it out of Cinch City,' Dannehar replied.

'You make it sound easy,' commented Stebbins dubiously.

'Just play along, do as I told you and you'll be plumb surprised,' murmured Dannehar. Whereupon he lapsed into silence and apparently dozed.

About fifteen minutes later, Marshal

Oskin and Deputy Dick Meader appeared in the passage, the younger lawman bearing a tray of food while the marshal carried a ring of keys and his unholstered sixgun. As the marshal unlocked the barred gate, Cephas Dannehar stirred into life and sat up on the bunk.

'Well, howdy, Slim. It's high time I sampled this superior grub you've been boasting about,' he greeted affably.

'Oh, it's good stuff, Cephas,' said Slim Oskin, taking up his position in the passage with his gun levelled through the big, barred gate of the cell. 'A generous plate of nourishing stew with some bread and an equally generous hunk of apple pie with good coffee. Cinch City knows how to extend hospitality – except to weasels like Mr Stebbins, here. Salt pork and beans are good enough for him.'

Dick Meader handed out the food and two sets of eating irons then stood close to the open door, holding the tray. The two prisoners ate with gusto, Dannehar obviously relishing his serving of food more than Stebbins enjoyed his.

Both Oskin and Meader slackened their vigilance a little as the prisoners concluded their meals and neither paid any particular attention to the way Dannehar rose and took a couple of steps closer to the standing deputy as he emptied his plate. Likewise, Stebbins, finishing his food, stood and walked towards the deputy as if to hand him the plate.

Dannehar afterwards had to give the shifty Stebbins grudging credit for his quick thinking and his speedy response after Dannehar spurred his action with a quick nod. The youngster dropped his plate and sprang forward, whipping his hat from his head and thrusting it forward to bury the young lawman's face in the interior of the headgear. He shoved the totally surprised Meader backwards while Dannehar snatched the sixgun from the deputy's holster as he scooted back on his heels.

'What the hell?' gurgled Slim Oskin from the passageway as he levelled his weapon through the bars to where Cephas Dannehar was administering a swipe across the jaw to quieten the young deputy as he lurched against the wall. Dannehar then swung the sixgun around quickly to cover the marshal beyond the barred barrier.

'Don't let loose with that gun, Slim, and we'll all get out with a whole skin,' he advised Oskin. Then, to Stebbins, 'Quick, kid, into the office for our guns!'

'By God, Cephas, put up your gun or I'll drop you for sure whether you're my old partner or not!' spluttered the outraged Oskin, who still held his pose impotently, his gun directed at Dannehar.

Stebbins bolted out of the cell, crossed the narrow passageway and entered the office while Dannehar stepped out into the passage, keeping the purloined weapon levelled at the marshal. The two stood there, each facing the other's gun. From the cell came a groan as the deputy, sprawled on the floor, began to recover from his rough treatment.

'Too bad you forgot the old hat trick, Slim,' grinned Dannehar. 'We first worked it on Sheriff Slaughter's deputy back in Tombstone in the old days, remember? Oh, quit waving that gun at me, you blamed old fool. You know damn' well you won't shoot me any more than I'll shoot you. I hate to treat you this way but I have urgent business in the Nations and I can't delay here in Cinch City.'

'Blast it, Cephas, get back in that cell or I'll let fly at you! I have a position to keep and I ain't letting any prisoners escape,' blustered Oskin. At that point, Cal Stebbins emerged from the office carrying two gunbelts with holstered Colts. He handed one to Dannehar.

'Here's yours, Mr Dannehar,' he said, with a new respect in his voice.

'Thanks, kid,' said Dannehar. Then the shifty youngster quickly lost his new-found respect because Dannehar smote him over the head with the deputy's sixgun, causing him to drop senseless to the floor. To Marshal Slim Oskin, standing openmouthed with levelled gun, he explained, 'He might be inclined to cling to me and I can't be saddled with a ranahan of his kind. You can take care of him while you're looking after your deputy. I'm heading over the street to collect my cayuse from the livery stable. No hard feelings, Slim. Here's to meeting again in happier circumstances.'

Dannehar made a hasty exit from the building with Oskin hooting after him, 'Dammit, Cephas, I'll come after you, you blasted sidewinder! I'll come after you!'

Buckling on his belt and Peacemaker as he went, Dannehar made quick tracks across the rutted street, now becoming shadowed by the gathering dusk. At the livery stable, he found only a languid youth reading a dime novel.

'I've come for the black bronc lodged by

Marshal Oskin,' said Dannehar. 'Has he been fed and watered?'

'Sure, mister. Your saddle and blanket are in the stall with him. You got Marshal Oskin's say-so to take the cayuse?'

'Oh, sure. He's given his full approval,' grinned Dannehar who was already in the stall, speedily and expertly saddling his horse.

Ten minutes later, he was riding at a smart clip along Cinch City's rapidly darkening street. As he passed the office of the city marshal, that furious official was standing in the doorway waving his Colt at his old companion of the trails but making no attempt to fire.

'Blast you, Cephas!' he was bellowing. 'I don't care how far into the Nations you go, I'm coming after you! I'll get even with you for this!'

CHAPTER TWO

INDIAN TERRITORY

Dannehar made a steady night ride and reached the Red River, separating Texas from Indian Territory, with the first fingerings of dawn light. The river lay, snaking and glistening below him as he eased his mount down a ridge towards blossoms of yellow light marking the windows of Sawberry's Store. Dannehar gave a grunt of satisfaction. It had been a long time since he rode this country and he was unsure as to whether Old Sawberry and his rickety commercial undertaking might even be still in existence. At least, it seemed the ramshackle wooden building was still there beside the ford which gave easy passage across the river even though, through the law of averages and the ravages of weather, it should have disintegrated years ago. As for Old Sawberry himself, he was the kind of leathery ancient who might well be immortal, so Dannehar fully expected to see him behind the counter-cum-bar over which he'd been dealing provisions and drinks since soon after the War Between the States as Texans liked to call it.

He was not disappointed. The wrinkled old-timer, seemingly hardly changed by the years, was leaning on the scuffed boards of the counter, wearing the same greasy hat, aged by unknown decades. Old Sawberry, like the activities of his store, appeared never to pause for sleep. Activities at that moment were subdued. There were only a couple of nondescript men in range gear, drinking at a corner table. Both had slightly suspicious demeanours but that was never unusual in the motley personalities who replenished supplies and slaked their thirsts at Old Sawberry's place, the way-station along the tangled trails which crossed the Red River into the Indian Nations.

Dannehar eyed the men from under his hat-brim, taking in their faces and their dress and conjecturing that they were wondering if he was a Texas Ranger or perhaps one of Judge Isaac Parker's deputies from Fort Smith, Arkansas, who had ranged far from his usual jurisdiction in pursuit of a fugitive. Or maybe they're thinking I'm just another hard case, drifting into Indian

Territory, which is what I figure this pair are themselves, he concluded.

Old Sawberry, with the air of one who is never surprised, observed, 'I'd say you were Cephas Dannehar if I hadn't heard he was shot dead in Denver or El Paso or some such place.'

'You heard wrong, Sawberry,' grunted Dannehar, noting with the tail of his eye the way one of the drinking pair nudged the other at Sawberry's mention of his name. 'But a man often mishears things. It's many a year since I was over this way but I heard you'd managed to improve your grub in the meantime. But, then, I could have mis-heard.'

'Grub here is what it always was, take it or leave it,' said Sawberry. 'I improved the stable out back, however. There's decent straw, water and feed there, too. I always did have more concern for horses than for the general run of my fellow men.'

'Good. I'll put my horse up while you're fixing hash, beans, coffee or whatever you can offer,' said Dannehar, turning and striding for the door.

He found that, true to his word, Old Saw-berry had fitted out the lean-to stable quite respectably and, while he was attending to

29

his animal, he heard the jingle and tramp of departing horses. The two drinkers had apparently picketed their mounts on the further side of the store from where Dannehar had hitched his bronc, which was why he did not see the animals on arrival. Now the pair were departing into the widening dawn, seemingly going towards the ford over the Red River and he suspected it was a hasty departure, spurred by his arrival on the scene.

He returned to the interior of the store and found that Old Sawberry had acquired the services of a plump and impassive Mexican woman cook who emerged from the kitchen behind the counter bearing pork, potatoes, beans and coffee which, with a set of eating irons, she placed on the table vacated by the two men.

Old Sawberry, still leaning on the counter, watched Dannehar sit down and begin to eat. Surprisingly, the quality of the food had improved considerably over what was on offer on his previous visits and he complimented Old Sawberry on that fact adding, 'I hear there's a heap of drifters heading out this way, like the pair who just lit out. Maybe it's the fame of your improved grub that's bringing them.'

Old Sawberry shrugged. 'There's all kinds of ranahans coming out this way, that's true enough.'

'And going over the ford into the Nations for some reason, as I hear it,' pressed Dannehar.

'True enough again, but I don't know what's attracting 'em into Indian Territory. I just fix 'em up with grub and whatever else they need,' answered Sawberry.

'You reckon they're Sooners?'

'You mean the jokers who sneak in to steal the land from the Indians sooner than wait for the government to pass a law to permit 'em to do so? Sure, there are some Sooners and they're plenty rough but there's another kind, too.'

'Like the pair who just left? The kind who look like gunsharps?' asked Dannehar, eyeing Sawberry over the rim of his coffee cup.

'There's plenty of that kind but I don't ask questions. I guess I'm just plumb uninformed.'

You're nothing of the kind, you tight-lipped old buzzard, thought Dannehar. You know plenty about the trafficking in these parts just as you know damned well that I wasn't shot dead in Denver or El Paso or any other place because I wasn't entirely un-known to fame in recent times – even in this back-end of nowhere.

He finished the meal, ordered a shot of whiskey, disposed of it then, still occupying the table and comforted by the warmth of the liquor, tilted back his chair, planted his feet on the table, tipped his hat over his eyes and announced to Sawberry that he was about to take a half-hour nap.

'You're welcome,' said the old timer from his lounging place. 'Matter of fact, I'm figuring on adding a wing to this place to provide sleeping quarters. By way of ex-panding business, you know.'

'Well, I reckon there's call for it,' mur-mured Dannehar from under his hat-brim. 'What with all them Sooners and whatever else kind of ranahan is drifting through here into the Indian Nations, intent on some-thing about which you're plumb unin-formed. Into the bargain, a new section of building would help hold up the rest of the place.'

Old Sawberry began searching for a suitably caustic response but a gentle snore from under Dannehar's tipped hat caused him to abandon the effort.

The sun was well up in the sky when

Dannehar headed his bronc away from Sawberry's Store and splashed into the ford. He rode easily through the stony-bottomed shallow spot of the Red River, left Texas in his backtrail and emerged into what the official maps described as Indian Territory, known colloquially as 'the Indian Nations'. Here dwelt an amalgam of Indian folk, chief among them the Five Civilized Tribes who, in the 1830s, had been forcibly transplanted from the lush lands of the south by Andrew Jackson's government.

Distinct from the nomadic hunting tribes of the Great Plains and the north-west, the southern tribes had been settled farmers for generations, living free under tribal custom with the more prosperous, even owning slaves. The old Indian-hater Jackson and the interests backing him wanted their lands, hence the government policy of removal to the far off, alien and largely empty region which on a distant day would become the proud state of Oklahoma but which would first become Indian Territory.

The removal was done by bribery, by coercion, by lulling reluctant tribal chiefs into agreeing to highly dubious treaties through liberal use of whiskey and sumptuous meals and by outright force. Escorted by the United States military, the southern Cherokee, Choctaw, Creek, Chickasaw and Seminole Indians travelled the long, bitter distances henceforth called the Trail of Tears. They went on foot for mile after mile and again for mile after mile by boat along the various rivers. *En route* their numbers were depleted by sickness, weariness and by the condition which might simply be called broken heartedness.

Now, with the end of the nineteenth century almost in sight, the displaced tribes and their descendants were settled in their towns on the government land grants which became the Indian Nations, living by a mixture of traditional custom under their tribal councils and of law and civil government patterned on those of the United States. There was still danger in Indian Territory. There were outsiders who wanted to get their hands on portions of this land. Someday, the government would give the word for legal settlement of much of it not yet legitimately apportioned, but, sooner than wait, gangs of armed, determined adventurers – the Sooners – came in, defying the law. In addition, there were motley drifters, men wanted elsewhere, taking refuge in the Indian Nations, gunmen ready to hire themselves out and a riff-raff of horse thieves and illicit whiskey dealers.

Surveying the wide vistas before him that bright morning, Dannehar gave a rueful grin and the sight of this country automatically caused his old arm wound to throb.

Dannehar was unlikely to forget his first experience of Indian Territory and the circumstances which took him there. Though aged only twenty, his intelligence and coolness under fire had elevated him to the rank of corporal in Rixby's Mounted Guard, a Texas volunteer cavalry unit which had fully tasted the blood and horror of the Civil War since it erupted in the spring of 1861. Now it was the summer of 1863, a bitter period for the southern Confederacy. In one week in July, the Confederate bastion of Vicksburg on the Mississippi was pounded into surrender by unyielding northern forces and a daring thrust far into northern territory by the brilliant senior Confederate commander, Robert E Lee came to grief after three bloody days at a Pennsylvania township named Gettysburg. This defeat brought to many southerners something they scarcely dared acknowledge openly: that the war had entered its last stage and there was no hope for the now badly impoverished and militarily depleted Confederacy.

Corporal Cephas Dannehar and his fellow Texas troopers felt they might be doing something more useful elsewhere rather than going on detachment to the obscure command of the equally obscure General Douglas Cooper in the hazardous lands of Indian Territory. Cooper, with a mixed force containing many Indians who were allied with the Confederacy, was charged with dislodging the Union forces under United States' General James Blunt from north of the Arkansas River to secure the frontier strong point of Fort Gibson and hold that region of Indian Territory for the rebel south.

Tattered and ill-fed by this stage of the war, Dannehar's detachment found Cooper's force, with its ranks of Cherokees, in no better case, but burningly determined to fight. Soon after Rixby's Mounted Guard arrived, the unit was in action and, as if on cue, the rain started, forceful, soaking rain which swept in pelting surges over the plains. In the midst of it, the two forces clashed at the Arkansas River, in a thundering maelstrom of action. And the Confederates quickly realized that the bulk of Federal fighting was being done by a pushing and tenaciously effective regiment of black soldiers.

With his head bent against the curtain of slashing rain, Dannehar had only an obscure view of what was going on ahead of him but he realized that the Federals had crossed the river and were spilling into the left flank of the Confederate force. He urged his mount onward into the thick of the blue uniforms, screeching the rebel yell and swinging wildly with his sabre. A hail of mine balls was loosed from the Union troops, causing Dannehar to duck forward and almost bury his face in his horse's mane. Then, before he realized that the animal was actually on the bank of the river, he found himself being pitched from the saddle as the horse slithered along a slant of mud, down towards the rain pelted stream. At the same time, a musket ball slashed through the left sleeve of his tunic, inflicting a burning sting to his upper arm.

Then he hit the mud with a thump which gusted the breath out of him and he went rolling down the slant helplessly to plunge into the river. With hardly a chance to gulp for air, he went under the surface, aware that his left arm appeared to be useless. He floundered up to the surface with his sound arm milling in an attempt to swim but immediately began to sink again. He seemed to be in a world of his own, only dimly aware of the battle raging above him on the lip of the river but only too conscious of the fact that he was drowning, impaired by his injured arm and the weight of his equipment.

Abruptly, he was conscious of a splashing presence beside him and of something grabbing his collar. Just as his strength was about to give out, he felt himself dragged back towards the bank. Trying to help himself and his rescuer by working his legs in a swimming action, he was hauled to the muddy bank and dragged clear of the water. Spluttering and snorting, he sprawled on the mud and felt his rescuer flop down beside him, also gasping heavily. Above the rise of the bank dinned the cacophony of the battle, something proceeding in a world detached from the lower reaches of the declivity in which the two men lay, fighting for breath.

At length, Dannehar managed to control his breathing.

'I'm obliged to you, mister,' he gasped. 'I

was about to go down for the third time.' He turned to look at his rescuer, sprawled alongside him. He saw a sodden uniform, a Union blue uniform with sergeant's stripes and the gleaming wet face of a young black man, capless and with a mop of crisp curly hair.

'Don't mention it, Corporal,' panted the enemy sergeant above the racket of the battle. 'I got tipped over that ridge up yonder in the thick of this ruckus. Next thing I knew, I saw you rolling into the river. Had to do something about it. Saw a youngster drown when I was a kid. Never want to see it happen again.' He paused, gulped air and added, 'I feel strongly about drownings. The youngster was my brother.'

'Hell, we're supposed to be killing each other,' murmered Dannehar incredulously.

'Sure. That bunch up yonder are killing each other and I figure we'll have to join in any minute. Damned if I want to kill you, though, after dragging you out of the drink,' growled the Union man.

'Damned if *I* want to kill *you*,' said Dannehar. 'What do they call you?'

'Sergeant Abel Aubert, First Kansas Coloured Infantry. And you?'

'Corporal Cephas Dannehar, Rixby's

Mounted Guard, Texas, detached to General Douglas Cooper's command – and not much liking it.'

'Can't say I much like the business in hand either, but I figure we both have a job to do according to the way we perceive things,' commented the black sergeant, who plainly had a pedantic turn of expression.

'I'll remember you. I owe you a good turn or two,' said Dannehar. 'I reckon we should scramble up this mudbank and get back into the fight.'

'Sure, but let's not finish each other off when we're involved,' grinned the Federal sergeant with a show of pearly teeth. 'I reckon you need attention for that wound as soon as you can. We'd best sneak up into that mess of noise and smoke and join our respective sides again.'

'And let's be sure nobody sees us hob-nobbing with each other. The officers on my side and yours are just as ornery as each other. They'd have the pair of us shot,' grunted Dannehar. He thrusted out his hand and it was grasped by the sergeant. 'Damned if I ever met a better man in this whole blamed war,' he said.

'Who's to say we won't come out of it living and breathing and meet again someday?' grinned the sergeant. 'We can hope for such a development, anyway.'

They parted, putting distance between each other before making their dripping and sodden way up the rain-pelted mudbank to plunge back into the action, each finding a place in the heaving masses of smoke-choked blue and grey. Dannehar, unhorsed, picked up a musket from a fallen Confederate and one-handedly clubbed his way through a knot of Union blue until he was swept back on a surge of mingled rebel infantry and cavalry as the southern line broke and retreated from the river in confusion. That day was won for the Union by General James Blunt's brigade in which the First Coloured Kansas regiment played a valiant part and the whole of Indian Territory north of the Arkansas River was lastingly secured for Abraham Lincoln's government.

The historians would write up the action under the title of the Battle of Honey Springs.

'Honey Springs, what a hell of an occasion!' murmered Dannehar ruefully. He rubbed the sleeve which covered a deep, white scar. 'And it didn't do a damned thing for the south right after Gettysburg had knocked us punch-drunk.'

He was riding through tumbled, rocky country bordering the river. It was sunny and peaceful, perhaps deceptively so because, under a smiling face, Indian Territory could be violent. There was varying law here, some enforced by the United States Indian Police and administered by the tribal magistrates of the Indian settlements. However, these arms of justice operated only within the Indian population. Non-Indians came under the eyes of an assortment of sheriffs and marshals and even through an overlap with neighbouring Arkansas. There, at Fort Smith, Judge Isaac Parker was the ramrod of a squad of marshals who ranged far and wide through Arkansas and the Indian Nations.

Parker, famed as a hanging judge, had an iron fist and a steely determination. It was whispered that some who died on his gallows might not have had the fullest justice, but it was not something to be uttered within the hearing of the judge or his marshals.

Well, for all the lawmen wandering the Nations and for all of Judge Parker's badge-toters, there's still deviltry of some kind up around Rapid Creek mused Dannehar as he approached a small stream. He halted to give his bronc its first drink since crossing the Red. After leading the animal to the water, he sat on a rounded rock, fishing a creased letter from the back pocket of his jeans as he did so. He unfolded it and began to once again read the words penned in a good hand:

'Dear Mr Dannehar,
It's been a long time since 1863 and that big fight at Honey Springs but I guess you might still recall me. I was Sergeant Abel Aubert in those days and I certainly remember Corporal Cephas Dannehar and the circumstances of our meeting. I saw your name not so long ago in a St Louis newspaper in consequence of you being a town marshal who settled some lawlessness in Arizona. A good time before that, I saw another report concerning you. You had again distinguished yourself in law enforcement.

'It's only fair to say that both reports made reference to your being very skilled with a gun and hinted that, at least in your younger days, you built a reputation as a gunfighter. I became a schoolteacher after the war, so I strove pretty hard to keep the youngsters in my care free from romantic notions about gunfighters, but circumstances in these parts caused me to think again. I might have been critical once but now I'm asking for your help.

'We need a gunfighter here at Rapid Creek. We're a pretty tolerant community as you might guess from my being appointed schoolteacher. Folks are mostly Indian with some whites and a few blacks, all striving to build a decent place to live. Recently, some murderous men have moved in to terrorize us.

'What law there was here went crooked and we are so isolated as to be beyond the reach of any other really effective law—'

At that point in his reading, Cephas Dannehar jumped as a rifle shot blasted out of the high-piled jumble of rocks behind him. A bullet *whanged* within an inch of his right ear and smote a boulder close enough to him to send chips flying into his face even as he instinctively threw himself forward to the ground, unholstering his Peacemaker as he went. He rolled over into the sheltering lee of a gnarled rock and faced the direction of the shot.

'Damned backshooter!' he growled. 'You're somewhere up in the high rocks. Show yourself, mister!'

He was painfully aware that whoever was trying to kill him was armed with a powerful rifle while he had only a sixgun. Far handier would be the Winchester in his saddle scabbard, secured to his drinking bronc. The animal, spooked by the shot, had now danced in fear some little distance along the stream.

'Dammit, mister!' Dannehar growled again. 'You're up in the high rocks, looking down on me. Maybe you aim to pin me down and play the waiting game, then pick me off when it pleases you. You're putting me into a hell of a hole.'

He hugged the ground, keeping his sixgun concealed lest the sun touched it to give a betraying glint to whoever was watching his position from the rocky ridge. His gaze travelled the rocks, seeking just such a glint from that quarter. He saw nothing but speedily drew back into cover as another rifle-crack blasted the air. A bullet arrived with a whining *zing,* only just missing the sheltering rock. Risking another look around his cover, Dannehar saw a drift of blue smoke against the far rocks where his would-be killer was holed up.

He blasted two shots at it, knowing he was fighting blind with no hope of hitting the rifleman but intending to provoke him into firing again to betray his position more precisely. At once another rifle report shattered the echoes, this time from further along the line of jumbled rocks. Another distant curl of smoke marked the location of whoever fired.

Damn! He couldn't have travelled that far along the rocks without my seeing him, thought Dannehar. There must be two of them, each holed up at a different position. Unless they run out of ammunition, they could keep me pinned down forever. They've got me hogtied and damn near branded.

More out of stubborn defiance than anything, he triggered another couple of bullets towards the rocks at the same time reminding himself that, against these odds he needed to conserve his ammunition.

Then another rifle shot blasted out of the high rocks, but no bullet came close to Dannehar's position. Hardly had the echo of the report clattered away than another rifle-crack came from the same quarter. Again, no bullet disturbed the man sprawled behind the rock near the margin of the stream. He lay there, trying to fathom the significance of the fact that the last two shots definitely came from yet another position, betraying a third rifleman.

The last shots were followed by a long, tension-filled silence then Dannehar raised himself a little, trying to take in a broader view of the rock cluster and thinking that with a trio of would-be assassins eyeing him from that quarter he was in an even worse fix than he had imagined. He saw no sign of life on the rocks and no further shots came.

Then a well-known voice sounded thinly across the divide between the rocks and his cover hollering, 'You can come out now, Cephas. There were a couple of 'em trying to get you. Those last two shots were mine. I finished 'em off!'

'Doggone,' gasped Dannehar aloud. 'Slim Oskin! How the hell did *he* get here?'

He rose slowly and bewilderedly to see a familiar skinny figure emerging from cover among the far rocks and begin picking his way down the tumbled landscape to walk towards him.

'You're sure getting old, Cephas, letting me get the drop on you so easy in Cinch

City then allowing a pair of no-account saddle-tramps pin you down that way. Hell, I wonder you managed to live this long without my guiding hand,' roared Oskin as he approached. 'They were out to make buzzard meat of you for sure.'

'What the Sam Hill are you doing here, Slim?' shouted Dannehar.

'Coming after you, like I said I would, you double-dyed rattler,' responded Oskin. 'A damned good thing I did, too. I don't know what you did to that pair back yonder but they sure had a down on you – and a couple of Winchesters levelled at you.'

Grinning, he came closer to Dannehar.

'You're a long way off your jurisdiction and not even in the state of Texas, Slim, but I can't say you don't have proper cause to take me in,' observed Dannehar.

'Damned if I want to do that, Cephas,' said Oskin as he reached his old partner. 'I aim to join you in whatever you're up to here in Indian Territory.'

'What? But you're marshal of Cinch City. I assaulted your deputy, slugged your prisoner and escaped your custody!'

'I *was* marshal of Cinch City,' said Slim Oskin, seating himself behind the rock which had sheltered Dannehar who joined him in leaning against the rock. 'I walked out on the job. Let's say I was getting jaded anyway. You effected a change in me. Let's say you started me yearning for the old times and the old antics when you pulled that hat trick on young Dick Meader.'

'Just walked out?' echoed Dannehar. 'What about the town council who seemed so blamed important to you?'

'The hell with the town council. They're a bunch of stuffed shirts who didn't pay me enough anyway. Young Meader can take over the job. He's efficient enough.'

Dannehar blew out his cheeks. 'Phew! Don't you have other responsibilities? In all the years since we last met didn't you get respectable? Didn't you get yourself a wife and kids, maybe? And a home?'

For a moment, Oskin looked crestfallen. 'Hell, Cephas. You know there was only one girl all those years ago. There could never be another.'

'Sure, I remember Helena, back in Arizona – and the damned fever that carried her away along with a lot of other people,' murmured Dannehar. 'You mean you stayed footloose all those years?'

'Sure. I was footloose at heart, though the job of marshal of Cinch City was one of many attempts to settle,' grinned Oskin, looking like a mischievous schoolboy. 'Oh, I aimed to get you when you lit out from my jail right enough. I was mad as hell. But when I watched you disappear out of Main Street, I got plumb nostalgic for the old days and the way things used to be.

'I went through some kind of regeneration right there on the doorstep of the gaol. There you were, splitting the wind for the Nations and obviously headed for something interesting and there was I, mad as a hornet at the way I'd been fooled. At the same time, I was admiring you for having the same old spirit that once set us to hell-raising. Then I saw that I was probably growing a paunch and was on the way to becoming a stuffed shirt myself.'

'Well, that beats all,' grinned Dannehar. 'You just up and quit on the spot?'

'I took time out for a last public duty and dragged that Stebbins joker back into the cell – he was sitting on the floor, holding his head and groaning,' Oskin explained. 'Then I comforted young Dick Meader with a slug from my private bottle because he was plumb dazed by the way you slammed him back with that hat trick. I went to the rooming house to shove a change of clothes into my warsack, settled my rent with Mrs Schultz, collected my cayuse and took after you.'

'It beats all,' repeated Dannehar. 'Strikes me you're a damn sight more irresponsible than you were years ago. Good thing you are, though, remembering the favour you've just done me. What did you make of the pair who were out to bushwhack me? I figure they might be two saddle-tramps I noticed when I stopped off at Old Sawberry's place. They sure showed some interest in me when Sawberry called me by name.'

'Reckon you're right. Two fellows in cowpuncher duds yet with that touch which gives you the notion that they could easily be up to no good. They're lying up there now. I figure we should cover their corpses with rocks,' said Slim Oskin. 'If whatever law there might be here, or one of Judge Parker's marshals drifts by, there's sure to be trouble.'

'And it could be murder warrant trouble,' confirmed Dannehar. 'My cayuse has wandered off along the stream and yours must be picketed up near those rocks. We'd better collect them then tend to our bushwhackers.'

'What's that slip of paper lying on the ground?' interrupted Oskin.

'A letter. I guess I dropped it when the shooting started,' said Dannehar, retrieving the folded missive. 'It's the reason I'm here in Indian Territory. Long ago, I was helped out by a man and said I'd help him out in turn sometime. Probably his last paragraph says it all.'

He began to read aloud from the point at which the shooting disturbed him:

'So many people are just plain scared there's no real hope of holding out against the intruders without someone to ramrod them into the determination to make a stand against the bad characters, who bid fair to overrun this section of the territory. By all accounts, you're still an effective fighting man and that's what we need. I'm asking you plainly if you'll come and put some spirit into folks who are fast running out of hope and some of them have, indeed, run scared off their holdings. In the finish, it's sure to mean some hard struggling.'

'He writes an eloquent letter, this friend of yours,' commented Slim Oskin.

'He sure does, considering he was a sergeant on the wrong side of the war – your side.'

'Well, that's all the more reason for me to throw my gun in with you,' grinned Oskin. 'Us Union men have to stick together. Anyway, on your recent showing, I'm not sure you're safe in getting involved in big-time trouble without my guiding hand. But I have to allow that, for a blasted rebel, you always were a man who'd stick to a promise.' He gave a short laugh. 'Hell, poking our guns in on behalf of the oppressed! How many times have we done that in the past? It'll be just like old times, Cephas. Damned if I don't feel as if I never turned thirty. I figure I'm losing the beginnings of that paunch, too.'

He moved off in the direction of the tumbled rocks to retrieve his horse and there was a new spring his lanky legs. Dannehar ranged down the stream to find his bronc, then led the animal back towards the rocks to join Oskin.

He considered his old partner, striding ahead of him, swinging the Winchester he had employed so effectively against the would-be assassins.

'You blamed lanky streak,' he murmured with a crooked smile. 'It's my good luck you showed up and my good luck you never lost any of your triggersavvy. And, though I'll never say it to your face, it's better than good luck that you're partnering me again, considering what we might be sticking our noses into.'

CHAPTER THREE

HOLE-IN-THE-WALL

They found the first of the luckless snipers sprawled face-down among the rocks, his head drilled by Oskin's rifle bullet. He was a slim young fellow in scuffed range garb and boots which had seen much wear. Even before they turned his face up to the sun, Dannehar recognized him as one of the pair he had encountered at Old Sawberry's tumbledown establishment. The face, for all its youth, had the pinched look of hardship.

'Looks like he's known hard times,' murmured Dannehar, not without some sympathy. 'That's the way of it now, what with the big land companies eating up the ranges that once were open and the old cowmen's ways being shoved aside.'

'Oh, sure,' said Oskin as he began to search the pockets of the dead man's buckskin vest. 'Times are changing and getting damned hard for all of us, and you and me, who grew up chasing cows, know it as well as anyone –

but we don't lie in wait to bushwhack strangers. There's got to be a reason behind this, Cephas. They sure enough weren't set on killing you just for any grub money they found on you. There's not a damned thing on this joker to give any identification. Only this little purse with six bucks in bills, a few coins and the makings for his smokes. Not even anything in the way of a letter to give a name.'

The second corpse was discovered some little distance away. As Dannehar expected, he was the second of the saddle-tramps from Sawberry's and he was drilled through the head as neatly as his companion.

'I have to hand it to you, Slim. You did a neat job of despatching them,' praised Dannehar.

'Nothing to it,' said Oskin dismissively. 'I heard shooting from the far side of the rock outcrop, giving away their positions. It didn't take any special Indian skills to sneak up behind 'em and look down on 'em from a higher point, and I could also see you and the hole you were in. They were so danged intent on their bushwhacking they never knew I was there. I still don't find any pleasure in doing what I did. They're some mothers' sons – and pretty sorry looking ones at that.'

The search of the second body again produced a few dollars, Bull Durham tobacco, cigarette papers and a battered pocket watch. When flicked open, its dial-cover was found to have an engraved line on its inner surface: 'To Sergeant Walter Kearton as a mark of respect from his platoon, 17th Illinois Volunteer Infantry, 1865.'

'This fellow's too young to have been in the Yankee army,' commented Dannehar. 'Maybe he inherited from his old man. At least, it gives us a name: Kearton, but it means nothing to me.'

'On the other hand, he could have stolen it from some unfortunate if bushwhacking travellers was the stock in trade of this pair,' observed Slim Oskin.

As with the earlier corpse's belongings, they dutifully returned the items to the man's pockets, then went in search of the dead men's horses, finding them hobbled some little distance away behind slab-like rocks to which they must have been led by their walking owners on account of the tumbled nature of the rock flooring. They were stringy animals, both bearing worn El Paso saddles, which spoke of Texas. There were the usual cow-country trappings:

ropes, bedrolls, empty rifle-scabbards and saddle bags which bore nothing other than shaving tackle and some beef jerky which was the only property pocketed by Slim Oskin. 'It'll only attract buzzards and we're plumb short of grub for the trail ourselves,' he commented.

Examination of the animals revealed no brands to suggest they were stolen. They were unsaddled and stripped of their bridles and trappings then turned loose, Dannehar and Oskin knowing they would wander first to the water to drink, then to find grazing in the open country and doubtless to eventually take up with a herd of mustangs. The pair then humped the saddles and trappings back to the corpses and performed a ritual of piling rocks on the bodies which they laid out complete with their sixguns and rifles, following the strict observation of not robbing the dead. The saddles and trappings were placed on the cairns of rocks as markers.

Slim Oskin produced a small, flat notebook and Dannehar watched as, with a stub of pencil, Oskin wrote:

'To whom it may concern, particularly United States Marshals, officers of the US Indian Police or other peace officers. The two unknown men interred here were shot by James J Oskin, formerly town marshal of Cinch City, Texas, who discovered them in the act of ambushing with deadly weapons Mr Cephas Dannehar, who was travelling in the course of his lawful affairs. Oskin and Mr Dannehar are willing to give an account of this incident to any properly authorized peace officer or justice of the peace if required.'

Oskin ripped the page from the notebook, folded it and slipped it inside the saddlebag crowning one of the cairns of rocks.

'Slim, for a man who suddenly desired to quit the peace officer business, you're a stickler for the niceties of procedure,' observed Dannehar with a wry grin. 'And you sure made that "Mr Cephas Danneher, travelling in the course of his lawful affairs" sound plumb respectable.'

'Got to do things properly,' grunted Oskin. 'It's expected in these changing times. It's why the job of town marshal was getting to be a chore – too much paperwork and giving accounts of everything creeping in.'

Chewing on the strips of dried beef, they trudged out of the tract of rocks to find their horses.

'Having undergone your peculiar conversion from the lawman's life, how was it you showed up in such an opportune way just as those two gents were giving me the best of their attentions?' asked Dannehar.

'Well, I figured you'd head for the Nations by the well-travelled way which more or less follows the Old Texas Road, so you'd probably cross the Red by the ford near Old Sawberry's place. But I know this Red River border country better than you do and there's another, quicker backtrail into the Indian Territory, though the river is deeper so your horse has to swim the river,' explained Slim Oskin. 'It's the owlhoot trail, used by gents on the dodge, and it brings you around the back of the ridge of rocks which splits the backtrail from the old trail you travelled. I heard shooting, climbed the rocks to come up behind those two, pinning you down.'

Mounted, and heading north, Dannehar gave an ironic chuckle. 'By thunder, Slim, you and me riding side by side again! Darned if it isn't like old times.'

'Sure is,' said Oskin. 'I got an overpowering nostalgia for the old days when you pulled that same old hat trick we pulled in Tombstone so long ago. But, in the old days, we made sure we had full bellies and this beef jerky reminds me that because of my hasty departure, I have nothing in the way of grub in my warsack and I'll wager you're in no better case.'

'Too true. You knowing the Nations as you do, have you any ideas as to where we can find some grub and maybe a bed for tonight, between here and Rapid Creek?' asked Dannehar.

'Well, this close to the old owlhoot trail, there's Gunstock. It's a sinkhole of a hole-in-the-wall town and you know what that means in Indian Territory.'

'Sure, it's neither an Indian nor a non-Indian town where there's likely to be crooked law or no law at all and a haven for outlaws, horse-thieves, liquor peddlers, Sooners who aim to steal land and the rest of the unsavoury gentry,' Dannehar said.

'Yeah, Gunstock lies in a hollow, almost totally hidden, and it's a place where I'll have to watch my back,' responded Oskin. 'Around these parts, you might be known by reputation but not by sight. Your peace officer days were spent mostly in the southwest but we're not too far from Cinch City and a whole bunch of dubious jaspers know me from there. I could be courting trouble by being in Gunstock.'

Dannehar laughed. 'Well, you've been getting damned monotonous with your eternally telling me how I set off the old urge in you to be on the trail and in action again with the hat trick I pulled on your deputy. So, if you run into trouble in this hole-in-the-wall town, I suppose you'll be ornery enough to blame me for it. Even so, let's get there pronto before we starve to death.'

They were riding through pleasantly green country, with undulating hills to the west. The faintly marked trail reached a fork, one arm of which swung away towards the hills and appeared to be lost in a stand of oak. Slim Oskin jerked his head in that direction.

'This way to Gunstock. The town is in the hills on the far side of the trees,' he said.

They took the westward arm and rode steadily, penetrating the cluster of trees to emerge in a fold in the land. A couple of miles ahead, a drift of smoke indicated the presence of a town. A space of riding brought them to where the trail ahead widened to become Gunstock's single street. At first view, the settlement was an unprepossessing collection of clapboard and log buildings, mostly warped and withered. A few slanted false-fronts to decrepit looking stores indicated that, in its earlier days, Gunsight might have had ambitions towards respectability, but everything now looked to have slithered badly. A few sluggish figures moved around the boardwalks, all seeming to share the town's lethargy.

'Not much of a town,' commented Dannehar as they entered the rutted street.

'It never was and I suspect it never will be. It's every inch a hole-in-the-wall, a catch-all for every owlhooter who wants to make himself scarce,' answered Slim Oskin. 'Take a look at some of the gentry on the boardwalks.'

Dannehar was already doing so with the habitual wariness he employed whenever he entered a strange town. His years of pursuing an off-and-on peace officer's career had made him some lasting enemies. There could always be someone who remembered him and desired to settle an old score. Among the thin populace, he saw down-at-heel men who had doubtless been cowhands, now suffering through the economic changes that had come to cattle-raising; the usual flotsam such as those who fancied the west would offer golden opportunities but were now in hard luck because money had become generally tight; those who had the look of horse thieves or just petty thieves and Indians who had drifted away from the social structures of the tribal settlements.

One man in particular took his attention. He was leaning against a hitch-rack outside a slanted clapboard building which declared itself through an ill-lettered sign to be a saloon and billiard hall. He was a scrawny cowpoke type, wearing a black sombrero and ragged range gear with wide chaps on his legs and a Colt .45 at his hip. From his leaning position, he followed the two new arrivals with an intent gaze.

'The guy in the black hat over to my right is interested in us,' Dannehar murmured. 'Can't say I recognize him. Have you seen him before?'

Without moving his head, Slim Oskin noted the watcher at the hitch-rack.

'No, but he'll know us again, all right. He's taking a good, long eyeful.'

'Evening is drawing in, so what's our move – find someplace to sleep, then eat?' suggested Dannehar.

'Sure, I never had the doubtful pleasure of overnighting in this gopher-hole, so I can't recommend any hotels but I figure they'll all be as bad as each other. There's one just along the street we could try,' Oskin suggested. 'As for the grub, I guess it'll be as unsavoury as everything else in Gunstock but we'll have to chance it.'

The hotel called itself the Palace of the Plains, but only the most impoverished of royalty could ever acknowledge it as a palace. Its narrow hall had faded trappings with a few decrepit chairs with greasy upholstery. A fly-blown portrait of George Washington hung on one wall. He was always a safe choice in Indian Territory: Abraham Lincoln or Jefferson Davis would be sure to create ructions from one or another faction. The desk was a dusty structure crowded into an alcove and behind it was a wizened, bald little man who looked as if he might himself date from the era of that same George Washington. He looked almost eagerly at Dannehar and Oskin as they tramped along the ragged carpet with ringing spurs, having hitched their mounts outside.

'You want rooms, gentlemen?' he said in a husky voice, which gave the impression that he had not used it to welcome guests for some time. 'I can offer a single room each. Washing facilities in each room. I'm sure you'll appreciate the comfort after some hard travelling. As a matter of fact, you'll find some blessed peace and quiet here because things are a mite slack and there's no one else in the hotel. Normally, I'm crowded out with guests.'

'Yeah, I'll bet you are,' grunted Oskin in a stage whisper.

The little man, who was probably slightly deaf, appeared not to hear him.

'Finest hotel in the fair city of Gunstock, gentlemen. You couldn't have made a better choice,' he said. 'I'm Otto Kroll by the way. I own the place.' He was already selecting two keys from a board behind him. 'Rooms six and seven, next to each other. Not large, but I'm sure you'll find them satisfactory.'

'Next to each other. I hope the walls are thick because I'm sure you snore like a hog,' observed Oskin in his mischievous stage whisper.

'Right up the stairs, gentleman,' said the proprietor of the Palace of the Plains. 'You'll find a livery stable right along the street and an eating house just opposite.'

The rooms proved passable with beds which, if not luxurious, looked acceptable enough to men who had been long in the saddle. The pair returned to their horses, toted their saddlebags up to the rooms, dumped them and locked the rooms. They installed their animals in the decidedly run-down livery stable then crossed to the eating house.

Evening shades were sifting down now. The air was pleasantly warm and yellow lamplight bloomed from odd-shaped windows along the street. Tinkling piano music and raucous songs sounded from the saloons. With wary eyes, Dannehar and Oskin considered the figures passing them on the street and lounging on the ill-lit boardwalks. In particular, they were interested in the man in the black sombrero who was so plainly curious about them when they arrived in Gunstock, but they saw nothing of him.

The grubby eating house was presided over by a lean, taciturn man who had a surliness which they were to find widespread in Gunstock and who obviously fulfilled all the functions of the establishment.

They settled for greasy pork, beans, potatoes, bread and coffee. The quality of the cooking suggested that the taciturn man might well have once been a chuck wagon cook to a trail crew, an impression strengthened by the fact that while his cooking was indifferent, he provided good coffee. The average chuck wagon cook's culinary horrors might be tolerated by the cowpokes but he invariably learned that he had to serve up good coffee in order to keep a whole skin.

'You know the deeper parts of the Nations better than I do, Slim. Do you figure we'll hit Rapid Creek tomorrow?' asked Dannehar as they ate.

'Yeah. A full day's riding will take us well into predominantly Cherokee country where Rapid Creek is located. Did your friend there tell you exactly what kind of trouble is shaping up around that region? D'you figure it's Sooners, out to grab land? They say there'll be a general opening up of public land to settlers before long – they even say Indian Territory will be made a state in time – but there'll always be those who'll come in, clawing for prime land sooner than wait for legal right to settle. You don't need me to tell you that there are roughnecks aplenty among them and they don't care about land already apportioned to the tribes.'

Dannehar shrugged. 'No. He didn't specify the threat but his letter made it plain the folks there needed the protection of a gunhand. He more or less asked me to go in smoking. I got the feeling things might be the way they were when the Lincoln County War bust loose in New Mexico or when the Earps and Clantons were brawling in

Tombstone. Times might be changing but maybe they're not changing all that much.'

'True enough. There's still a mite too much lead in the air all over the west,' agreed Slim Oskin. 'They want a gunhand in Rapid Creek, well maybe it's just as well that they have double that number on the way. Could be that one of us – and I'm not saying which one – is slowing up and needs the backing of the other.'

Dannehar gave a snort. 'You're not saying which one, but you're giving a broad enough hint, you snake. Need I remind you of my speed and slickness in overpowering a certain town marshal in a town called Cinch City? Need I remind you, too, how it so impressed the same marshal that he was inspired to throw in his hand as a lawman and take to the trail, as in the days of his youth?'

'All right, don't get tetchy about it,' grinned Oskin. 'Let's just say the ex-lawman has no regrets about it and is glad to be along. So let's go get some shut-eye.'

Back at the hotel, they strode past the desk where the proprietor was snoring in his alcove.

'I reckon we can take the measure of this place by the fact that we were not required to register,' commented Dannehar as they mounted the stairs.

'No point in registering in a hole-in-the wall like Gunstock. Just take a look at some of the gentry on the street. Hardly one of them would write his real name if he did register anywhere,' Oskin replied.

In spite of the run-down condition of the Palace of the Plains Hotel and the almost night-long noise from the street, the pair slept solidly in beds which were just about acceptable. In the morning, before checking out, they sampled more of the cooking at the same eating house where the good coffee compensated for the indifferent bacon, beans and pancakes.

At the hotel, they settled their bills with the gushing Mr Kroll who was certainly the most outgoing citizen of Gunstock they ever encountered and probably the only one with any civic pride.

'Visit us again, gentlemen,' said he. 'Gunstock holds a welcome for all the world.'

'Or at least that portion of the world that's on the dodge,' murmured Oskin, the aside being missed by the slightly deaf hotel proprietor.

At the livery stable, they found that their horses had been groomed and apparently well fed and bedded in clean straw even though the heavily bearded oldster who had charge of the place seemed none too bright and had the surliness which seemed part of the Gunstock air.

'Can't say I'm sorry to shake the dust of this place off my boots,' said Slim Oskin as they saddled their mounts.

'Nor me. I want to get to Rapid Creek pretty darned quick. Abel Aubert's letter made matters sound urgent and we seem to be making mighty slow progress,' complained Dannehar.

They rode steadily down the street, watching Gunstock coming sluggishly alive with the new day when Dannehar suddenly started and drew Oskin's attention to a man making his way into a clapboard-fronted saloon. He wore the wide leather chaps of a cowpuncher and a broad black sombrero. He was already unsteady on his legs. His back was to the pair of riders and he was unaware that he was under their scrutiny.

'It's the guy in the black hat who was so interested in us yesterday!' declared Dannehar.

'Looks like he's already had a drink or three,' said Oskin. 'And going into a drinking-den this early in the day means he must be pretty much a soak.'

'Hell, Slim, there was just something about the way he stared at us that got under my skin. I figure we should sidle up to that joker and learn something about him. Call it my old lawman's instinct but I have a feeling about him,' said Dannehar.

'Me too,' agreed Oskin. 'Let's pay him a visit.'

They eased their animals over to the saloon, dismounted, hitched their horses and shoved the batwing doors of the saloon open.

The place was almost empty with only a handful of customers of the habitual drinker type leaning on the bar. The man in the black sombrero was in the very act of taking hold of a shot glass of liquor being passed to him by a dull-faced barman.

Dannehar and Oskin walked up to him and leaned on the bar alongside him.

''Morning,' they said in unison.

The man turned drink-dimmed eyes toward them. Under his black sombrero, his face brightened and he gave a broken-toothed smile.

'Well, doggone, it's you two!' he greeted. 'I figured you were the pair when I saw you show up in town yesterday. I was aiming to find you sooner or later. Had some business to attend to in the meantime – a little drink or so, y'know.'

'Yeah, we noticed you and we figured you were noticing us when we arrived in town,' said Dannehar.

'Yeah. I told myself you must be Hart and Kearton, the gents we came here to meet up with. I figured Blewitt and me would catch up with you later,' the black-hatted one replied, at which Slim Oskin gave Dannehar's leg a meaningful nudge with the toe of his boot but Dannehar had already noted the use of the name of Kearton, inscribed inside the watch found on one of the dead bushwhackers. The man swallowed his drink with a single gulp, chuckled then waxed yet more voluble.

'It looks like this Rapid Creek affair will be some antic and I'll allow I'm sure looking forward to it. From what I hear, Dragon has the whole thing tied up and will move in pretty swiftly as soon as–' He interrupted himself with a hiccough, 'as soon as Reese and his crew clear out the opposition. It'll be the quickest clearing of a scrubby little Indian town off the face of the earth as ever was known. I tell you, I'll sure relish my part in it like I relished the money Dragon gave me in advance – relished it along with the liquor it provided.' He gave another tipsy chuckle. 'I hear tell you two gents are no slouches when it comes to backing rough play. Why, I tell you, when it comes–' He belched. 'When it comes to–' At that point, he swung his head around as the batwing doors flew open and a lean, middle-aged, black moustached man with a face contorted by anger burst in.

'There you are, Tatum. Hell, I might have known it!' he bellowed. 'Even at this time of morning, you're hoorawing around the saloons. You suddenly got too much money than is good for you, you drunken fool!'

'Howdy, Blewitt!' called the black-hatted man affably. 'Come on over and meet Hart and Kearton.'

The newcomer's mouth dropped open. 'Hart and Kearton be damned!' he exploded. 'Hart and Kearton are young guys, not a pair of dried-up old coots! What the hell have you been saying to this pair, you blasted barfly?'

'Not Hart and Kearton?' mouthed the drunk bewilderedly.

Blewitt, the man with the moustache, was staring at Slim Oskin. 'No,' he rasped. 'And the skinny one is marshal of–'

'Don't do it – you're drunk!' bellowed Cephas Dannehar. It was a stark warning to Tatum, the man with the black hat, who, realizing the stupidity of his loose talk, was clutching for his holstered Colt .45. With his mouth twisted into a panicky grin, he telegraphed his intention. At this close range, his move could only gut-shoot either Dannehar or Oskin. But, even as he shouted, Dannehar had his Peacemaker bucking in his hand. He triggered it, sending Tatum pitching back against the bar. He slithered to the floor, gusting a dying gasp.

Through swirling gunsmoke, Dannehar saw Blewitt swiftly drawing his sixgun and swinging its mouth towards him, but he fell back with flailing arms as Dannehar's pistol barked again. He was dead before he hit the floor and, in the curiously still moment which followed the speedy trigger-play, Dannehar found that Oskin, gun in hand, was side by side with him. Then Oskin swung himself around, so that the pair were back to back, covering the whole room. It was a stance they had employed in many tight corners in many places during their wilder, younger days.

'By grab, Cephas, I was beginning to think you were getting slow, but I was plumb mistaken,' breathed Oskin. 'I was out to get the second ranahan but you plugged him first, and pretty darned fast at that.'

They surveyed the bar room through the drifts of smoke. The few early patrons and the barman were standing frozen and round-eyed and two corpses lay twisted on the scarred boards.

Dannehar now thought of the repercussions of the drastic gunplay and what effect they might have on the efforts to reach Rapid Creek.

'What kind of law do you have here?' he asked the silent onlookers.

A tall, long-haired man in a worn broadcloth suit who looked like a cross between a failed gambler and a gunfighter who had hit hard times, spoke up in an educated accent. 'Law is hardly the word for it, friend,' said he. 'There's a marshal of a kind but he's mostly drunk and his deputies are not much better. This place is a hole-in-the-wall and its law is every bit suited to it. Saloon shootings are nothing new here.'

'Any of you see what happened here?' pressed Dannehar.

'I did,' confirmed the long-haired man. 'Both of 'em tried drawing on you and you wouldn't have stood a chance at that range.

You preserved your life and that of your partner, as you have a right to. Ain't no argument about that, as I reckon everyone here will agree.'

There was a general nodding among the assembly.

The long-haired man continued in his pedantic manner. 'Since that fellow with the moustache said one of you is a marshal from elsewhere, I figure what was between you had something to do with some trouble from elsewhere. None of it is any concern of mine. All I saw was a man defending himself and his partner fair and square, which is what I'll tell Gunstock's marshal if he sobers up enough to come asking questions – and, knowing him, he won't. For all any of this will make any dent in the affairs of Gunstock, you might just as well ride out of town without any further fuss. It'll just cost Gunstock the price of two burials in Boot Hill and nothing more.'

'That's about the way of things in Gunstock,' piped up another patron of the saloon, made bold by the long-haired man's talkativeness.

'And that's sure enough the way of a real hole-in-the-wall,' murmured Dannehar to his companion. 'The shooting was witnessed as plain self-defence, which means we can ride out of this place without any further ceremony.'

They holstered their weapons and strode for the street. Passing the contorted corpses, the moustached one looking like a saddle-tramp and the other, with his broad chaps, plainly a cow-wrangler who had hit hard times, Oskin commented, 'I'd like to know a whole lot more about those two and what they were involved in.'

Dannehar nodded and, when they were in the saddle and on the hoof, with the last of Gunstock's straggling single street slipping into their backtrail, he said, 'Plumb peculiar that those two should be in the town. They were obviously expecting the pair we left back in those rocks. They were aiming to go to Rapid Creek for some deviltry and it's plainly organized deviltry at that.'

'Sure, and they left us with some names to puzzle over. Did you note 'em?' asked Oskin.

'I did,' nodded Dannehar. 'Reese was one, Dragon was another and that Tatum joker blabbed about clearing Rapid Creek off the map. Kind of gives us a picture of what is shaping up around Rapid Creek way.'

'Sure. It looks like somebody is building an

army to make plenty of trouble for your friend Aubert and his townsfolk,' said Oskin. 'I've heard of plenty of trouble in Indian Territory in the past, what with Sooners coming in to occupy the unassigned public lands before they have any right to do so, and occasionally run Indians off land they have occupied under the old treaties, and the antics of horse-thieves and whiskey-dealers. But I have a doggone funny feeling about this business we're getting into. It looks like something new.'

'It's big, too, and we're not *getting* into it – we've been in it for some time in a peculiar way,' Dannehar grunted. 'I can explain that Blewitt guy knowing you were a lawman by his passing through Cinch City at some time, concealing the fact that he was a gun-packer from even your hawkish eyes. But how did Hart and Kearton know I was headed for Rapid Creek and so lay up to bushwhack me? How many more trigger-tripping, flotsam-like, drifting saddle-tramps and cowhands hit by the hard times are headed for Rapid Creek? And who are Reese and Dragon who're obviously offering gun-money?'

'More than that, they're sending it in advance,' said Oskin. 'You heard that drunk

Tatum talking about how he got his drinking money.'

'Damned if it don't smell more like the start of an old style range-war the more I get wind of it and innocent folk stand to suffer,' Dannehar said. 'That's why we have to get to Rapid Creek pretty damned quick.'

'Yeah, pretty damned quick,' echoed Oskin.

Acting instinctively in unison, they touched spurs to their mounts and speeded up their progress.

CHAPTER FOUR

GUNS FOR THE CHEROKEE

They rode north, heading for the Blue River country, keeping up a smart clip until well away from Gunstock.

Ahead of them was the bulk of Indian Territory, divided into various components making up the 'Nations' of the Southern tribes forcibly removed from lush lands under the harsh policies of Andrew Jackson's government and herded by the military along the gruelling and death-haunted 'Trail of Tears' to be resettled. This was turbulent country, still finding its way. It was a bolthole for outlaws seeking obscurity and there were others, the Sooners, who, hopeful of making a new start, harboured land-grabbing avarice against the many acres technically controlled by the government and unassigned to any owner. There were men with dark schemes, often willing to employ others to do their villainy – even killing – for them. There was a floating riff-raff of motley incomers such as those who dealt in bad whiskey among the Indians to whom liquor was forbidden and horse-thieves and cattle rustlers.

The Indians, settled through government treaties, lived under double discipline. There was their tribal law, administered by the traditional elders, and a form of civil justice of judges and magistrates which they had adopted from the United States, of which no Indian was yet a citizen.

Eventually, Dannehar and Oskin saw the tell-tale drift of woodsmoke which betokened the presence of a town and they headed for it.

The township sprawled under the sun, a collection of board and log buildings, aligned along two sides of a wide, dusty street. It had a neater, cleaner and altogether more honest look than the outlaw-infested Gunstock, huddled guiltily in its fold in the hills. A board beside the trail, which eventually became the town's street, bore a carved Indian symbol and a carefully lettered legend: *Choctaw Nation: Town of Blue Flats.*

'It looks a mite more healthy than our last port of call,' commented Dannehar.

'And more than a mite more sober, liquor being banned in the Indian settlements,' said Slim Oskin. 'And we can find a store here where we can buy some trail-grub which'll be more palatable than anything from that Gunstock gopher-hole.'

They entered the street, noting its sparse population of men with black hair hanging in long braids and women in bright skirts. Leaning against a hitch-rack were two youngish, lithe looking men in flat-crowned black hats. Each wore a buckskin vest over a spotted shirt and on each vest, a metal badge glittered. Each man carried a Henry rifle and, though they held lazy poses, the pair were clearly watching the newcomers closely.

'Indian police,' said Oskin. 'And they're mightily interested in us.'

'So would I be if I was an Indian police-man, knowing the kind of gentry drifting into the Nations and seeing the likes of you and me arriving in a peaceful Choctaw town,' grinned Dannehar. 'There's a store over yonder we might try.'

They angled their mounts across the street to the boardwalk, swung out of their saddles and hitched their reins.

The interior of the shop was cluttered with all manner of household necessities and there was a rich, mingled smell in which coffee and freshly baked bread were detectable.

Behind a counter loaded with a variety of foodstuffs stood a middle-aged Indian and a plump woman whose neatly braided hair was prematurely white. Their copper-skinned faces were impassive, but their dark eyes warily considered the newcomers with their dusty signs of hard travelling and their shell-belts and holstered Colts.

Dannehar and Oskin nodded affably to the couple and the couple returned the nods.

No sooner had they approached the counter than they heard a ringing of spurs behind them. The two Indian policemen had entered and planted themselves one on either side of the street door. Sunlight streamed in from the street, showing that one man had a sergeant's stripes on his shirtsleeves and striking brightness off the fittings of the Henry rifles which they held nonchalantly and onehandedly. Each man leaned lazily against a door jamb.

'Mr Sam Black Oak here has tolerable good vittles for men on the trail,' said the sergeant in a firm and friendly voice. 'There's good bread for men on the trail here, too. Tolerable good bread. Mrs Black Oak here bakes it herself. Worth taking a supply if men were on the trail. In case you don't know this country, this is the Choctaw Nation. Men on the trail ride some distance north and over the Canadian River and they're in the Creek Nation.' He lifted his rifle lazily, clicked the hammer then unclicked it and lowered the weapon.

The message was plain enough: *buy some supplies then clear out of the Choctaw Nation – whatever you have a mind to do, do it elsewhere.*

'Thanks,' nodded Dannehar. 'We'll take your advice.' Then, to the storekeeper, 'I figure a loaf of bread would be a start and some coffee and a couple of cuts of salt bacon.'

'And some of that new-fangled fruit in tin cans if you have any,' put in Oskin with relish.

They made their purchases and, watched by the two Indian policemen from the door of the store, packed the food into their warsacks, mounted, rode out of town and resumed the trail north.

'I've been thrown out of some towns in the course of my shameful life, but never in such an elegant way as that,' said Dannehar.

'Can't blame the policemen for watching their jurisdiction closely. The Indian farmers and ranchers and townsfolk throughout the

Nations have been plagued by ruffians and thieves long enough. At least they gave us time to collect some trail-grub,' Oskin pointed out. 'Obviously, there's not been time enough for any word of our ruckus in Gunstock to come this far but, to them, it's a white matter and they have no jurisdiction over whites.'

'Still, being conscientious, as they obviously are, they've probably noted us. In due course, they might tell white officers they've seen us,' said Dannehar. 'With so many hard-case ranahans drifting into the Nations through this Reese and Dragon business, whatever it is, I can't think they haven't been noticed by the Indian police. There might be no-account white law in Gunstock but if the Indian police tag us as a couple who killed there, who're now on the loose in the Nations, they might press the white law enforcement in the wider Territory to put out warrants for us. The clock could be ticking against us.'

'Hell! Quiet down, Cephas,' shuddered Slim Oskin. 'You're making me see Judge Parker's gallows in Fort Smith looming ahead!'

They made steady northern progress, crossed the Blue River at a shallow point and, after watering their animals at the river as the sun descended, headed for the fringe of a stand of oak on the crest of a rise and began to make a night-camp.

A sandy declivity in the land close to the sheltering trees made a suitable place to build a fire and there they broke out a skillet from Oskin's warsack, bacon, bread and eating irons and cooked a substantial supper. After eating, they spread their bedrolls under a tranquil, star-sprinkled night sky.

'Darned if this doesn't bring back memories of the old times,' commented Dannehar drowsily just before he set about disturbing the air with his snores. 'How many times did we make a night-camp all over the west?'

'Too many times,' snorted Oskin. 'And don't remind me of the old times. There were too many night-camps where we had trouble with rattlesnakes and trying to bed down on soggy ground, not to mention the occasions when we were plumb short of grub and money. I don't thank you for getting me into this at my age.'

'What?' spluttered Dannehar. 'You got yourself into it. You could have stayed in Cinch City, lording it as town marshal and getting fat around the middle. When I came along, I brought a whiff of the old days with me and you just couldn't wait to get on the trail with me all over again. You're just as fiddle-footed as you were at twenty, you cantankerous old horned toad, and you'll be no different at ninety-nine.'

From his bedroll, Slim Oskin answered with a rumbling snore.

In the morning, they consumed the last of the bacon and bread and Oskin showed how well stocked his warsack was by producing a can-opener which allowed them to eat the fruit which had so taken his fancy. Then they saddled up, returned the short distance to the Blue River for the animals to drink, then resumed their wayfaring northward.

Evening was nigh when, after traversing the Creek Nation without incident, they edged into the Cherokee Nation and were approaching Rapid Creek, when the tail of Dannehar's eye caught sight of a tell-tale silhouette on a rise in the land some distance off.

'See what we have up yonder?' he asked quietly.

'The rider who's watching us? Yeah I see him,' said Oskin, squinting at the hump of land.

The distant horseman held a still pose

against the darkening sky, looking like an equestrian statue. Then he and his mount slithered back to disappear behind the crest of the rise. Yet Dannehar and Oskin knew he was still there.

'Is he alone or are there others and who are they?' queried Dannehar.

They kept their eyes on the far rise without seeing any further sign of life but feeling that they were under constant scrutiny. In some subtle way, the atmosphere here in the Cherokee Nation seemed to be more tense than that of the neighbouring Indian nations. As men whose vigilance was sharpened by years on dangerous trails in lawless country, Dannehar and Oskin sensed the unmistakable whiff of imminent danger in the air.

They rode onward, then suddenly they saw a stark sight which, outlined against the garish crimsons and yellows of the setting sun, had an eerie loneliness. It was a deserted log building which appeared to have once been a homestead. Spurring their animals to a trot, the pair rode to the ruin and halted in front of it.

Somebody had sweated to create this place and lavished care on it, the care that an obviously hopeful soul wished would result in a comfortable home where youngsters could be raised and where the land could be tilled. But now it was devastated – rendered to blackened timbers and ashes by hungry flames.

It had plainly been burned out some little time before. The charred wood of the ruined walls and the tumbled mounds of ashes had been weathered by at least one winter and a ravaged and woebegone tract of land beside the ruin seemed to have once been a family vegetable garden which had been churned by hoofs.

Cephas Dannehar cuffed back his hat and grimaced with disgust.

'Remember what Aubert said in his letter about there being trouble, even murder out this way?' he asked his companion. 'This wasn't much of a place, just somebody's attempt to make a small farm but it looks as if they were denied a decent chance. We're within easy hail of Rapid Creek and on Cherokee land. Unless I miss my guess, this is the kind of thing Aubert meant when he wrote about deviltry here. I figure this was a deliberate burning.'

'I agree,' said Oskin, narrowing his eyes to focus them on something he spotted among the ashes. He dismounted and strode into the ruins, stooped and picked up a rusted kerosene can.

He held it up for Dannehar's scrutiny. 'I reckon we've found proof, too,' he stated.

'Yeah, I think I see the pattern. Just the same as driving nesters off the cattle ranges in the old days,' mused Dannehar. 'I figured those days were over and done with.'

'Elsewhere, they may be but there's something damned ugly going on up at this end of the Nations,' grunted Oskin.

'And Reese and Dragon, whoever those gents may be, are behind it,' said Oskin. 'I'd say we're getting close to what we came here for.'

They took to the trail again, pushing across country of gentle hills which had a fresh and richly fertile appearance under the spring-time sun. Promising land for ambitious and hardworking farmers to exert their efforts on – if left in peace to do it, thought Dannehar.

The sight of the charred ruin intensified the sense of foreboding which had accompanied them almost from the point where they had entered the Cherokee Nation, and the pair rode on in silence into the gathering gloom – a silence abruptly broken by the crack of a rifle. A bullet *zinged* close to Cephas Dannehar's head as the report of the weapon clattered over the enfolding hills.

Instinctively, Dannehar and Oskin dropped into a forward crouch, their noses almost touching their saddle-horns to reduce their chances of becoming sitting targets. Each grabbed for his sixgun. Another rifle shot blasted and another bullet screamed close. Then came a drumming of hoofs.

From the direction of the point where they first saw the watching horseman, a dozen or so riders, dark, menacing forms against the shadowed slants of land, were riding down upon them. All were waving rifles. One was out in front of the others, clearly leading the charge. The dozen followers speedily strung themselves into line abreast behind the leader like cavalrymen, beginning an encircling movement to surround Dannehar and Oskin. Cephas Dannehar, an old cavalryman himself, saw the efficiency of the move.

'Hell, Slim! They're getting us corralled too damned easily!' he bellowed frustratedly.

The leader of the rapidly advancing riders made a small figure in the saddle, looking little more than a youth, with a banner of long hair streaming back from under a broad-brimmed hat. This rider yelled, 'Get the hell out of here, quick! Get off Cherokee land and stay off!' It was a high pitched, determined command.

'Dammit, he's nothing more than a boy!' growled Oskin.

'But a hell of a good cavalry commander,' snorted Dannehar. 'His troop has got us hogtied, slick as the devil!'

Dannehar and Oskin had no choice but to rein up as the riders drew in and formed a tight circle around them, halting their steaming and snorting mounts. In the gathering gloom, the pair could see braided hair and dark Indian eyes which were no more welcoming than the menacingly flourished rifles.

The horse of the long-haired youth who had headed the charge was spurred forward and its rider stated in level terms, 'If it's not already plain to you gun-pilgrims, we don't want your kind here. We're giving you a better chance than others of your kind have given our people, so turn around and ride out while you're still breathing.'

'Hold hard, Fox,' rumbled a rich voice from among the knot of riders. 'Unless I miss my guess, this here is ex-Corporal Cephas Dannehar, sometime gallant soldier in the service of the State of Texas, and he brought a friend along.' The rider urged his steed forward and the encircled pair saw a black face under the brim of his sombrero, offering a welcoming grin.

'Ex-Sergeant Abel Aubert, of the Kansas Coloured Infantry,' gasped Dannehar.

'The very same, if older, a mite fatter and a damn sight balder,' responded the other. 'Excuse our rough and ready welcome and the commanding ways of Fox, here.' From his saddle, he extended a hand to Dannehar. 'Fact is we need direct measures to hold back unwanted intruders and the young fellows here have formed a defence squad.'

Dannehar shook Aubert's hand and nodded towards the horizon at his back. 'I can see the necessity of it if what we witnessed back yonder is the work of those intruders,' he said. 'This here is Slim Oskin. He was once in the Yankee army, too, but I manage to keep friendly with him.'

'Slim Oskin? Well, that's a name I recollect from the newspapers as well as your own. You made some contribution to law and order yourself, Mr Oskin,' said Aubert, dancing his horse around so he could shake Oskin's hand.

'Well, I made a modest contribution,' conceded Oskin.

'I reckon this is our lucky day,' grinned

Aubert. 'We sent out for one noted gun and we got two. That burned-out property back yonder is an example of the dirty work of our enemies. They're pretty powerful but we aim to make a stand against them – right up to the last breath if it comes to it.'

'You seem to have formed a tolerable good cavalry troop as it is,' commented Oskin.

'But we still need you two gents with us to stiffen our resistance. We need generalship,' said Aubert. 'There are a set of mean lead-slingers on the other side. There was some bloodthirsty work from this bunch north of here only it was the Osage who suffered there. They had doubtful title to their lands and there was intimidation and banditry which, in the finish, helped by the work of crooked lawyers, drove them off their holdings. I heard later they regretted their lack of fighting organization and lamented not calling in a trustworthy professional gun or two. That's what made me think of Cephas Dannehar. I recall a promise you made in the thick of the battle at Honey Springs and I figured you were the man to stand by it, even after all these years.'

'Well, Slim and I witnessed something of the range-wars and know what they meant for people who were trying to live peaceable. We don't want to see that kind of devilment starting all over again. We're here to stand with you,' stated Dannehar levelly.

'Good,' said Abel Aubert. 'Come on down to the town for some grub. I never doubted you'd come so I persuaded the Tribal Council to make a house available for you. It's small but I reckon the two of you can share it easy enough.'

The riders formed a double column and spurred their animals into a brisk trot. With Aubert and the two new arrivals at their head, they rode into the gathering night. Eventually, they hit a trail and passed a board nailed to a tree. It bore a legend in Cherokee, the only Indian tongue with a written alphabet, devised by the great scholar of his nation, Sequoyah. Beneath it was a line of English: *Township of Rapid Creek, Cherokee Nation.*

Dannehar jerked his thumb at it. 'Got a right pleasant sound to it,' he observed. 'But we picked up hints about wiping your town off the map with people named Reese and Dragon behind it.'

An ironic chuckle came from Aubert. 'Reese is flesh and blood, all right, but Dragon isn't a person – Dragon is a company.'

'A company?' echoed Oskin over the tramp of hoofs.

'I see. One of those blasted big cattle companies who can't get their hands on enough land,' growled Dannehar. 'They're plumb poison.' He thought he perceived the pattern of it now: the significance of the gathering of trigger-tripping hard cases he and Oskin had encountered in Gunstock and possibly of the pair who had so mysteriously tried to bushwhack him soon after crossing the Red River. It was the old game of forming an army willing to run occupiers off coveted land by force. Such manifestations of raw frontier life, he thought, were rapidly passing with changing times.

'No, Dragon's business is not cattle – it's oil,' said Abel Aubert.

'Oil?' echoed Dannehar bewilderedly. 'I heard of land-grabbing for cattle graze, farming or gold, but oil is something new.'

The trail snaked down a slope of land and the subdued lights of the town came into the riders' view. It was dark now, a pleasantly warm darkness which should have made night travel in open country such as this wholly enjoyable. But there was a marked tension in the atmosphere which was emphasized when two figures, afoot, emerged out of the blackness. They carried Winchesters.

'It's OK, Lou, Bear. It's only us, going home,' Abel Aubert called. 'The two gents we scouted are a couple of friends, here to give us a hand.'

As the two sentinels slipped silently back to their posts, he explained to Dannehar and Oskin, 'We keep our scouts out all around the Rapid Creek tribal holdings with a string of riders ready to spread the alarm if any strangers who look like Dragon's gunslingers show up.'

'It worked in our case. I reckon you and your boys were ready to settle our hash,' grinned Dannehar.

From what the two new arrivals could see of the small town in the darkness, it was a compact cluster of small houses and stores. It was typical of the settlements of the Five Civilized Tribes, transplanted out of the south in the 1830s under Andrew Jackson's Indian Removal legislation. Dannehar and Oskin knew that, viewed in daylight, the town would hardly be pretty but it would have a proud spirit. For it was a Cherokee settlement and the Cherokee were a distinguished people.

Different from the demoralized Plains Indians who once hunted the buffalo and were now relegated to the reservations and dependent on government handouts, the Cherokee of the Indian Nations still held to their tribal traditions and the Tribal Councils held power within their communities. But, running in tandem with the councils' authority, were their versions of white society's civic institutions. In the south, before removal to Indian Territory along the bitter Trail of Tears, many Cherokee had been prosperous farmers and even slaveholders. In the great upheaval of the Civil War, they had hoped to stay neutral but finally threw in with the slaveholding southern Confederacy, forming such fighting bodies as the Cherokee Mounted Rifles. Yet, all these years on, the Cherokee of Rapid Creek had a black man as an obviously leading personality of their community – and a black man who had fought with the opposing army of Abraham Lincoln's Federals at that.

At a livery stable on the shadowed main street, Abel Aubert called on the mounted troop to halt and disperse and the newcomers' horses were installed in fresh straw and given feed.

'Come on up to my place and eat,' invited Aubert and they joined him in a walk towards a small log house with the black man leading his horse. It was then that his severe limp became apparent.

'What happened to the leg?' asked Dannehar.

'Shattered by a bullet soon after I had the pleasure of hauling you from the water at Honey Springs. I was left lying on the field only half conscious after you Johnny Rebels made your retreat. I had the good luck to be found by some Cherokee. Darned if they didn't take me back to their settlement and take care of me – and me a Federal sergeant. I decided right then and there that if I ever had a chance to help out those folks I would. Seemed to me the Indians had been given as bad a deal as us black folks. They even made it easy for me to sneak out of their little town and find my way back to the camps. A lame man is no good to the infantry, so I was mustered out. Made it back to my wife in Kansas.'

Aubert hitched his horse to the fence rail and they mounted the porch of Abel Aubert's house. 'Wife?' echoed Dannehar. 'You mean you were a married man when your outfit and mine tangled at Honey Springs?'

'Sure. I'd been married just a few months,'

said Aubert, ushering the pair through the front door. 'Come on in and meet my wife, Marietta. When they raised the coloured regiments in Kansas, I figured to join was the right thing to do and Marietta saw it the same way. When I got back to Kansas, there was damned near as much upheaval there as in the war. I found ways of getting the pair of us back here to the Cherokee folks for whom I'd formed an affection. I was never a slave, being adopted by intellectual white folks and I was always a reading man. So I figured I'd take to teaching school.'

'And he gives the kids a lot better education than they'd have in the official Indian schools,' declared a comely black woman with greying hair who appeared as they entered the main room of the house.

'Marietta, this here's Mr Dannehar, answering the call I sent out, and he's brought a friend along to give a hand,' said Abel Aubert. 'Can we rustle up a meal for them?'

'They're right welcome to sit in to supper,' said his wife. 'It's fried chicken with potatoes and greens and some apple pie later.'

'Sounds like the kind of supper I haven't had since I was a kid,' commented Slim Oskin zestfully and all but licking his lips. 'I'm beginning to be glad I found my way to

Rapid Creek.'

After the satisfying supper, with coffee served, Dannehar asked, 'What's all this business about oil being the cause of the trouble around here? I figured oil was just something quack doctors sold at country fairs.'

'That's snake-oil,' laughed Oskin. 'I declare, Cephas, there are times you sound like a man who never saw a newspaper from one year's end to the next. Don't you recollect how they first found oil in boggy land in Pennsylvania just before the big war? They sure enough used it as a cure-all at first then found it could be used in lamps instead of whale-oil. Some gent then discovered a way of drilling into the ground to bring it up in big fountains.'

'Oh, sure,' murmered Dannehar. 'I recollect a fuss because the Bible-reading folk figured all that black stuff coming out of the earth must mean they'd drilled into hell itself and there was such an all-fired scare, it put an end to the drilling. I thought it was all forgotten long ago.'

'Far from it,' said Abel Aubert. 'Drilling started up again because the big money men figured there were untold fortunes in oil and there were lakes under land all over the country, just waiting to be tapped.'

'Yeah, the big money men like to get their way with things,' mused Slim Oskin. 'I recall some talk of oil becoming important in future. Maybe, with the cattle business changing the way it is, oil will be the next booming commodity in the west? I heard whispers about the occasional land-grabbing ruckus because it was believed oil was under the earth. It sounds plumb ugly.'

'It sure is ugly to judge by that burned-out place we saw back yonder if that was the work of this Dragon outfit,' said Dannehar.

'It was Dragon's work, we just can't prove it,' answered Abel Aubert. 'That was Teddy Blackfeather's place. He was farming happily enough in his quiet way and a bunch of riders just swooped on him one night and burned him out. Teddy and his wife and three kids got away with their lives but everything he'd worked for was ruined. They didn't move in on his land. They just did it to warn the rest of us that they aim to have their way. It all happened right after Dragon men turned up and made offers to the Tribal Council for land here on the settlement. They claimed they found signs of oil seeping into the creek bottom from our land. Damned derisory offers they were, too, not that the Tribal

Council would sell out at any price.'

'You sure the burning was done by Dragon's men?' asked Dannehar.

'Oh, sure, the riders were masked, but they were led by a guy whose bulk gave him away. Teddy recognized him as a big guy known as Reese. We gather he's behind collecting the bunch of gunnies who're clustering around Dragon,' said Aubert.

'Yeah, that's a name we've heard before,' grunted Oskin. 'Quite a recruiting sergeant with Dragon's money, this Reese.'

'And burning out Teddy Blackfeather wasn't the end of it. A couple of our young fellows were bushwhacked on lonely trails soon afterward. It was plain murder and Dragon are to blame for sure,' Aubert replied.

Dannehar sipped his coffee thoughtfully and said, 'So the Dragon outfit is gathering its army and paying good money to gunnies from every which way. I suppose they're camped not too far away.'

'Across the creek at the other side of town,' Aubert replied. 'They're on public land but the creek marks the boundary of the Rapid Creek Cherokee holdings. Over where Dragon is camped there's the remains of an old town called Enterprise. Some early

Sooners set it up long ago and, as an enterprise, it failed. Some of our young men sneaked over the creek and scouted it out without being caught. It seems Dragon have taken it over. Their engineering bosses are there with a hell of a lot of drilling equipment – and a growing amount of gunslingers for companionship. It's damned near an outlaw town and Dragon sure enough means to mount an onslaught against us sooner or later. They're using scare tactics first, aiming to drive some of our farming families out, I guess.'

Dannehar thought back over the years to the squads of lead-throwers backed by crooked lawyers and twisted lawmen who had figured in the bitter cattle-wars and the battles to acquire land for railroad expansion. He remembered drunken Tatum in Gunstock who had been advanced gun-money and who blew it in saloons. He'd talked of Reese wiping out an Indian town. There was no doubt as to what the Dragon Oil Company was cooking up here at Rapid Creek.

'I guess the Indian Police can't really do much in a set-up like this, having jurisdiction only among Indians and being thin on the ground anyway,' commented Oskin.

Abel Aubert shook his head. 'No, and you know there's a certain kind of lawman who never worries overly about what happens to indians and who sneer at Indian judges and Indian law. There's a sheriff of that kind here and his deputies are no better. The whole bunch are on the take from Dragon, for sure. It's a powerful outfit with plenty of money for bribes.'

'And you're a long way from Judge Parker's civil administration over at Forth Smith but I figure there'll be some among the Dragon ranahans for whom the judge's marshals hold warrants and some who're ripe for his famous gallows,' said Slim Oskin. 'This Reese joker interests me. Can't recall any bad man who was specially fat, most of 'em were thin from poor rations. I'll just bet we know him from the old days under another name but he somehow chanced to fatten up. He sounds like he belongs to our generation, Cephas.'

'Well he's plumb poison. So are the whole crew of 'em,' said Aubert. 'After they started their incursions over the creek, we formed our troop of riders, based on the old Light Horse Troops the tribes organized for protection soon after the removals from the south. We aim to put up a strong defence

106

against 'em but the Tribal Council insists that we don't mount any raids in retaliation so as to keep the Cherokee on the right side of the law. We'll only fight in defence of our own land. And I say "our land" because Marietta and me belong here as much as any Cherokee.'

His wife had entered with fresh coffee. 'We sure do,' said she. 'We had a little daughter, our only child. She died at seven and is buried here on this land. This place and the Cherokee people are precious to us. I don't want to see any trouble but after what's been happening here, I know why Abel and the other men are setting up defences and why they brought you gentlemen in. I don't normally approve of gunfighters but I feel you're different.'

'Mr Dannehar and Mr Oskin have very good credentials, Marietta,' Aubert replied. 'They're just along to give the boys some generalship. It's needed with Dragon shaping up the way it is,' said Aubert.

The small house on the main street made available by the Tribal Council was modestly furnished and invitingly comfortable after the pair's horseback journeying. They made their way back to the livery stable to collect their bedrolls and saddle gear to make ready for a night's rest.

Humping their burdens along under fitful moonlight, Oskin observed, '"Generalship", that's the word the man used, talking about you and me. I like the sound of it, though you don't look much like General Robert E Lee, nor do you have his brains – and I'll allow he had brains, for all he was a rebel.'

'Well, I'll concede General Ulysses S Grant had brains, too, even if he was a Yankee,' responded Dannehar. 'I figure we'll need the brains of both of them because it's plain we're going up against big odds in bucking this Dragon outfit.'

'Big odds didn't faze either Lee or Grant and blamed if the prospect of it isn't bringing back that youthful feeling all over again,' grinned Slim Oskin.

CHAPTER FIVE

MENACING DRAGON

The council-house was a log building shaded by oaks and its cool interior was floored with heavy boards and sparsely fitted with functional furniture. The Tribal Council, mostly older men with seamed, copper faces, beaded shirts and braided hair, grey or snow white, sat with stolid dignity on a row of chairs with Dannehar and Oskin seated before them.

'You know you are welcome here,' said the chairman. He carried an air of ancient nobility seeming to speak of a time well before the Cherokee were driven here into the raw lands of Indian Territory. 'We know you are men who have administered the American law but we are suspicious of that law. We do not want the instigation of anything to bring the weight of that law against us.' He paused and waved towards a window. 'Out there hostile men are gathering and their eyes are on our land. You must understand that there are others who have very similar intentions: powerful men whose plans are more subtle. I mean men in government in Washington. They talk of passing laws that will cause the breaking up of the lands we have held since first we came here, driven by soldiers along the bitter trail. These lands, so deeply sacred to us, may be taken out of our ownership and parcelled out to new settlers. Already there is talk of forming this territory into a state, which will mean the destruction of much of our way of life. We oppose any form of statehood which will rob us.'

'We understand,' Dannehar assured him. 'Too often, promises have been made to the People only to be broken.'

The chairman nodded, taking note of Dannehar's use of the word 'People', the term by which all Indians referred to themselves. It marked him as a man of sympathy.

'We must never provoke retribution from the law of the white men,' rumbled the chairman. 'We will never sell our land as we made plain to those who came with insulting offers – but we will defend it.'

'As you have a right to,' said Dannehar. 'No right-thinking American will deny anyone the right to defend his home and family.'

'Just so, but there are those who are quick to claim there is evil in any Indian action. Plenty would still turn the soldiers on us if given an excuse,' answered the chairman. 'So, ensure that all your actions are proper. We trust you to guide our young men, some of whom have tempers of fire which is something we of the council understand for we, too, were once young. Do not lead them into hotheaded action off the limits of our own land but remember, we have seen murder done here by outsiders. So, if there is any invasion of what is ours, resist it. We trust you because our schoolteacher, who is a man of honour, recommends you as men of honour.' The elder raised his hand. *'Pado,'* he said, offering the Cherokee wish of good fortune.

This was the day after the arrival of the pair in Rapid Creek and, leaving the council-house, they were met by Abel Aubert who, having introduced them to the Tribal Council, had waited outside for them and was now on the way to his school.

Dannehar told him, 'I figure we need to put our heads together with you and your riders to make the defences firmer. First, though, Slim and I would like to look around the perimeters of the tribal holdings so we know where to act with legitimacy and where we must hold off.'

'And we'd like to have some idea of where the Dragon outfit is camping,' suggested Oskin. 'If they mount any attacks, we want some idea of where they might come from.'

'Ride over a couple of miles to the west. You'll see a grove of cottonwoods on a crest overlooking the creek,' Aubert advised him. 'The creek marks the boundary of our land. It's all unassigned land on the other side and that's where the Dragon outfit is. The town of Enterprise lies a mile or so west. Approach the cottonwoods from the far side of the creek and some of our boys will come out to meet you. They're camped in there, keeping watch on the land across the creek. They can't see everything on the other side because there's a bend in the creek that obscures much of the view, but a fair amount can be seen. There's every chance of spotting a raiding party before it crosses the creek to our side.'

The pair jogged off through the bright morning, enlivened by a pleasant breeze. They noted how the town evidenced a mingling of tribal traditions and those of pioneering nineteenth-century America. Amid the log cabins and clapboard buildings were clan symbols, totems and signs in the curlicues of the Cherokee alphabet, devised by Sequoyah, the intellectual father of his people.

They hit open country and headed in the direction of the creek, appreciating how the Cherokee, when forced to put down their roots in what was harsh untamed land, had employed sweat and determination and the skills learned through generations in the south to develop farmsteads where crops and cattle flourished.

But a new, thrusting force was stirring on the land beyond Rapid Creek threatening everything which the Cherokee, with their peaceful and hardworking aspirations, had created.

Talking long and earnestly with Abel Aubert the previous night, Dannehar and Oskin discovered that he had learned much of Dragon's background and what was feared most from the oil company was 'wild-catting' – aggressive speculation on promising land.

Dragon coveted the land of the Rapid Creek Cherokee and, having had its derisory offers rejected, had surely turned to the old brutalities of the cattle-war bullies with a dark-of-the-moon burning and a couple of bushwhackings, hoping to frighten the Cherokee into eventually selling. More drastically, backed by its army of gunnies, it might even stage a naked land-grab, moving on to the Rapid Creek holdings illegally, sinking a well and establishing a virtual private armed state there.

Dannehar and Oskin already had some inkling of the ultimate action contemplated by some gun-ruffians recruited by the mysterious Reese, men whose thinking was twisted by sheer anti-Indian blood lust – clearing the Rapid Creek community off the face of the earth.

They rode up rising land, topped by a distant line of cottonwoods and as they approached the trees, two horsemen appeared abruptly out of them and galloped towards them. As they drew nearer, one was recognizable as the long-haired Fox who had led the riders against them the previous evening. His companion was, similarly, a keen-faced young man and both carried side arms with scabbarded Winchesters at their saddles. They raised their right hands in greeting as they recognized the newcomers and hauled their spirited broncs to a halt.

'Abel suggests we take a look at the geography around here and get some notion of

Dragon's position,' called Dannehar.

'Sure, come on up to the trees,' said Fox. 'There's a bunch of us camped in there, watching the far side of the creek. Dragon doesn't know we're in there so we never show ourselves on the creek side of the trees. We always come and go from this direction, behind the trees.'

In the stand of trees, they found a further three of Rapid Creek's younger men, equipped with a couple of spyglasses. From the shelter of the timber, they could look down and across the swiftly running creek in its broad, muddy bottom, surveying the broad expanse of empty land on the further side. It was folded terrain, with waves of low hills and occasional clumps of timber. Over a distant line of hills there arose a thin drift of blue smoke.

'That's Enterprise, the broken-down old ghost town which was deserted until Dragon showed up and took the place over,' said Fox. 'We have a fairly clear view of the land between there and the creek and hope to see anyone from Dragon approaching to cross the creek to our land.'

'And they sure enough aim to do something of the kind,' said Dannehar thoughtfully. 'Otherwise, they wouldn't be hanging around in Enterprise. It seems they're dead set on drilling over on this side of the creek.'

'Yeah, they figure there's a lake of oil under our settlement and they want it,' commented Fox's companion.

'Which will mean hauling their equipment over the creek,' put in Oskin.

'There are some bends on the creek where the view is obscured by trees and along various stretches there are shallow points where they might cross in force,' Fox said. 'If they manage to sneak up on the creek by coming the long way around under the shelter of the low hills so we don't spot them from here, they might just cross, hidden by the trees.'

'So, it'll call for a tight watch along all of the creek,' said Dannehar.

'And being ready for a stand-off,' added Oskin.

The land sprawling beyond the creek held a tranquil and sunny aspect but the watchers were all too aware that it cloaked the crouching Dragon, brooding and waiting to pounce on the coveted lands of the Cherokee. Through a spyglass, Dannehar watched the far distant smudge of smoke, marking the ghost town occupied by the oil company and its bullet-throwers.

'If that's a broken-down and forgotten town, where do the ranahans on Dragon's payroll do their drinking and sporting?' he asked. 'Don't tell me a bunch of jokers of that kind with gun-money in their pokes sit around with their crocheting every night.'

'I figure they drift into Arrow Flat,' Fox told him. 'That's a town some way back of the hills beyond Enterprise. The law there will tolerate the Dragon crew – the county sheriff out that way has been bought by the company. The place is little more than another hole-in-the-wall town.'

Dannehar drew his mouth into a thoughtful line, a mannerism whose significance was not lost on Slim Oskin. It was a sure sign of some idea ticking over in Dannehar's mind.

That evening, with Aubert, some of the young defenders of the settlement and some of the tribal elders, held a conference at Aubert's home. They drew up a plan to tighten armed vigilance along the creek and to increase the numbers of youthful riders ready to move swiftly around the settlement at short notice in case of attacks on any outlying farms or homesteads. They based the structure of the mounted troops on that of the early Light Horse Troops of the

Indian Nations out of which grew the United States Indian Police.

After the dispersal of the meeting, Dannehar and Oskin lingered over the coffee-pot with Aubert. Oskin considered the pensive mood which had gripped Dannehar ever since scouting the land from the wooded crest.

'Out with it, Cephas. There's something rankling you. You're figuring on pushing something,' he challenged. 'I know the signs. You've got a burr under your saddle-blanket.'

'I keep thinking,' drawled Dannehar, 'that I'd admire to drift across that creek and take a close look at Dragon's set-up at this ghost town, Enterprise, and maybe even look in on the other town, Arrow Flat. Just to look at how things lie over there.'

'Not, of course, to cause any sort of ruckus, since the Tribal Council don't want anyone from Rapid Creek to step out of line owing to the way the law can be slanted against Indians,' said Oskin, raising a quizzical eyebrow.

'Of course not. Just to observe the enemy from a distance without revealing ourselves and maybe learn something about this Reese joker some way or other because I'm plumb fascinated by him. Fact is, the old cavalryman in me doesn't like a lull with nothing going on.'

'Well, you and I are sure to be recognized by some of the ranahans over there if we're spotted. Me especially, since some of 'em passed through Cinch City and I accommodated 'em for a night,' mused Oskin. 'Still, I feel something of the same inclination. Maybe it's the old soldier in me that's itching, too.'

The black schoolteacher grinned broadly. 'Damned if it doesn't sound attractive,' he said spiritedly. 'I've been feeling an itch, too.'

'Now, hold hard. You've got a lame leg,' cautioned Dannehar.

'Leg be damned – I can ride as well as any man.'

'And you have a wife,' said Oskin.

'Oh, Marietta knows I'll only fret if I don't get a chance to do something useful. She'll probably pack something tasty in the way of grub for our journey. Beside, I'm a sergeant and I guess I outrank the pair of you – so I'm coming!'

Dix Tynan was tough, ugly and smart. He was tall, blocky and with heavy shoulders. He had a high-beaked nose and sharp black eyes almost permanently scrunched through looking into distances under harsh suns and his complexion was pitted and scarred by years of hard living in wild places. He wore greasy riding breeches, scuffed boots and a bleached checkered shirt which had seen much service. He sported a holstered Colt .45. He was no gunfighter but, as chief field boss of the Dragon Oil Company, roughing it with hard-case characters for months on end, he packed the pistol as good insurance and, in the past, it had proved its worth in camp brawls.

Tynan was a thruster, a chancer and an achiever; a man who knew his business. And it was his business to establish drills on promising land and bring up gushers of that profitable new bonanza, black oil. To him, oil was the coming thing, the new wonder of the west and he believed it could bring riches as staggering as the Sacramento gold strike of yesteryear.

Oilmen of Dix Tynan's kind were called 'wildcatters', forceful, devil-be-damned pioneers in a new field. All too frequently, his kind had ambivalent attitudes towards laws. When it was safe to do so, Dix was among those who nudged aside aspects of law that hindered his accessing the black gold under the earth. When it came to opening up new fields, he was not averse to strong-arm coercion to force ranchers, farmers and Indians to buckle to Dragon's will. It all had to be done with an eye to loopholes to be exploited if matters ever reached a court – but the driving force of Dix Tynan's method was brutality.

As a breed, wildcatters were beginning to multiply as the oil industry got into its stride and Tynan was determined that none of them would outstrip him in the scramble for black gold here in Indian Territory.

Normally, Tynan's uncompromising methods kept him ahead of any competition, but some problems were arising in his present assignment. The attempt to purchase land from the Rapid Creek Tribal Council had been scornfully rebuffed, so Dix Tynan had turned the squad of gunnies loose.

Led by Reese, about whose true background very little was known, they had crossed the creek under the cloak of darkness and burned out a vulnerable farmstead. Two further raids followed. On each, prowling the tribal lands and narrowly eluding the vigilant squads the Cherokee had hastily formed, the Dragon gunmen surprised a couple of lone Indians on obscure trails and bushwhacked them.

Elsewhere, when these brutal measures had been followed by a further approach to the landowners, weighted by scarcely disguised threats of further depredations, the intimidated landowners usually yielded and accepted terms twisted in Dragon's favour.

Initially, Tynan thought his tough-minded outfit was on safe ground employing bludgeoning methods at Rapid Creek: the county sheriff had been squared by the company and he had no real jurisdiction over Indians, anyway. The Indian Police were thin on the ground in this portion of the Nations and, while the far-ranging US Marshals in the service of Judge Isaac Parker, over the border at Fort Smith, Arkansas, were distinctly dangerous, they had so far not come investigating after Dragon's bloody coercion on Cherokee land.

But snags were arising. Firstly, when Dragon's armed minions subsequently surveyed the Rapid Creek settlement from the creek bottoms, they usually spotted troops of mounted Cherokee keeping what was obviously a heightened watch on the creek margin. The indications were that the settlement would not easily buckle under to the oil company's strong-arming.

Secondly, there was a worrying development concerning the so-called security crew signed up by Reese. This largely unsavoury bunch of drifters, receiving gun-money from the company, had begun to find their encampment amid the tumbledown log and clapboard shacks of a played-out frontier town boring and irksome. True, they had availed themselves liberally of the wares of the illicit rotgut peddlers who constituted one of the curses of Indian Territory but, in the long run, they craved more. Then they discovered Arrow Flat, squatting a few miles away, beyond the hills.

It was a wide-open, scarcely civilized hole-in-the-wall. Such law as it had was crooked; it boasted saloons galore – and it had girls!

Once Reese's bunch of roughnecks with pokes heavy with substantial funds guzzled what was on offer in its smoky drinking dens and fell under the spells of the ladies who draped themselves, pouting and winking, over the rails of the upper galleries of certain houses, they headed in a beeline for Arrow Flat at every opportunity.

The situation was creating a headache for Dix Tynan. The big money men in Philadelphia who owned Dragon – and who had never been within a hundred miles of its front-line operations – knew nothing of the realities of life out in the field but wanted movement and profits from the Rapid Creek venture. They were not forthcoming.

Tynan's only visits to Arrow Flat were to pick up wires from its telegraph office, the nearest one in the locality. Constantly, they asked questions. What was happening at Rapid Creek? Why was there no progress? Why had Dragon not sunk at least one test well? Why was the company paying out a Niagara of money and seeing no return?

Every time Dix Tynan rode into the town, his anxieties multiplied. There were always some of Reese's hard cases to be observed, clearly on pleasure bent. Everyone from Reese himself down to a brash, mouthy kid, who was his youngest recruit, were squandering good time in Arrow Flat.

It did not stop there, for something like an epidemic was developing. The engineers and roustabouts – the technical men whose skills were needed to bring forth the gushers when Dragon finally did make inroads on to the Cherokee land – were beginning to be affected. Usually, they held themselves aloof from Reese's gang, seeing themselves as superior but, now, they too were drifting into Arrow Flat far too often.

Dix Tynan had always known the dangers of dealing with such specimens of humanity as Dragon found essential to its strong-arming. In his time, he had personally handed out a beating or two when drink cursed a camp and he had once been wounded when gunplay flared.

Things were getting out of hand at the Dragon establishment in the crumbling ruins of Enterprise. Reese, who was rumoured to be some half-forgotten gunman from an earlier day who had changed his name, had already shown himself to be big for his breeches. He and his minions seemed to have forgotten what they were there for. If the rot was not stopped soon, Reese and his gang would be calling the tune and running the camp. Dix Tynan had no intention of permitting that. He was in charge of this whole operation and he aimed to make that understood. At the same time, he realized that, so long as nothing was happening as to action on the work front, the irksome malaise would deepen and idleness would breed more drunkenness. He had to initiate a thrust to tap the reservoir of oil he believed to lie under the Rapid Creek settlement or continued idleness would end in his own firing.

This morning, he left the dusty room where he made his headquarters – it had once been a doctor's office and it was still equipped with some rickety furniture left behind when the optimistically named town of Enterprise failed – and he strode along the dusty track which had once been the main street. All around him were the trappings of oil exploration: carts and buckboards laden with sections of metal drills and oddments of wooden scaffolding for the creation of derricks. The *remuda* of workhorses swished their tails against the flies in a corral constructed in a vacant lot and bored roustabouts and some of Reese's men lounged on rotting, sun-warped porches.

The sight of this collection of equipment, idle and gathering dust, angered Tynan as he stalked the street with a storm of angry impatience surging in him. Throughout the night, an almost desperate plan had been forming in his brain – he would force the end of this impasse by bold, old-fashioned wildcatting. He was going to bring Reese and his crew to heel and put a drilling crew on to the land across the creek. Opposition from the Cherokee would be met as opposition elsewhere had been met by Dragon in the past – with armed force.

And it would be done forthwith.

He found Reese, loafing in the company of some of his gun-heavy henchmen, outside the rickety clapboard building in which he bunked. Dix Tynan did not like Reese at the best of times and, this morning, he liked him even less. He was a grossly overweight man with an unkempt beard and a Colt .45 holstered conspicuously under the overhang of his belly. There was a dullness about his seamed face and a bleariness to his eyes which suggested a session of hard drinking the previous night. A stub of cigar was between his lips and he shoved his jaw out in a pugnacious fashion as Dix Tynan confronted him. It was a gesture which suggested contempt and reflected an attitude which Tynan had increasingly come to resent.

Both men were cut from matching material: each had a craggy toughness and neither liked buckling down to anyone.

Tynan came at Reese head-on. 'This loafing around is going to stop – pronto!' he stated flatly. 'A crew is going over the creek tonight. Your gang are going to support it. If it comes to a fight, it comes to a fight, so get your guns together and keep your bunch sober.'

Reese looked almost affronted. 'Go across

the creek?' he echoed.

'Yeah. Go across the creek in force and get down to business,' snorted Tynan, waving a hand toward the loaded wagons. 'What do you figure all this gear is here for?'

'Them Indians keep a pretty tight watch over on their side of the creek,' objected Reese. 'We nearly got caught last time we were over there and, after that visit, they'll be a damned sight more watchful.'

'And your last visit was a matter of killing on a back-of-the-scrub trail. What was it for? Just for fun? Just because you and your crew don't like Indians? Do you think the company is paying you to go Indian-hunting for pleasure?' Dix Tynan almost spat out the words. 'No, you meathead, it was to soften them up; to scare them into understanding who's taking charge around here and show them we aim to have our own way and to have their oil.'

'They might put up a hell of a fight,' said Reese.

'Yeah, they might. Not so long ago, we were hearing war talk from you and your bunch about wiping out the whole boiling of Cherokee over yonder. What happened to all that fire in your guts? Got quenched by the rotgut, I suppose. Got kissed away by the painted dolls in Arrow Flat where so many of your unearned dollars are being frittered away!'

'It ain't going to be easy,' wavered Reese.

'No. Nothing in the oil-grabbing game is easy,' said Tynan. 'Get this straight, Reese. We've loafed long enough and now we're acting fast. We're in on the game early in this part of the Indian Nations and we aim to capitalize on it. Pretty soon, Washington will form this whole region into a state and where will that put the Indians, with all their precious tribal traditions and all the concessions and land grants they've had? Out in the cold, that's where. When real progress begins in these parts and big money rolls in, no one will give a damn about the tribes no matter how much they squawk. Things will be going all our way, maybe in just a few months' time, and Dragon means to be at the front of the crush. Get your men together and keep them off the rotgut. I have to talk with the men who really matter in this outfit.'

He bestowed a parting hostile glare upon Reese and the motley collection standing around him, the grizzled veterans of yesteryear's frontier villainy and the surly, mouthy kid to whom Tynan had taken an instant dislike at first encounter. Pretty soon, he thought, if this country was opened up to statehood and waves of new settlers flooded in, specimens such as these would, along with the Indians, be swamped out of existence by a tide of progress. Until then, however, he'd make sure they earned their gun-wages from the company. It was a case of having to because the last wire from Dragon's headquarters was almost scorching his back pocket. It was scathing in its criticism of the field crew's idleness and it demanded action.

He strode off to call a meeting of the engineering brains making up his exploratory team.

In his headquarters, Tynan gathered his technical crew around him and spread out a large map of the Rapid Creek region on a shaky table.

'We've hung around long enough,' he stipulated. 'We move tonight when it's dark. We'll haul our gear to the creek by way of the hollows between the hills to give the Cherokee less chance of spotting us from the other side. We'll head over the shallows near the bend right here.' He stabbed a finger on the snaking line of the creek. 'There's a line of concealing trees there and we'll stand a good chance of getting over without being seen. That point is very close to where we first found evidence of oil seeping out of the Cherokee land. Immediately across the creek is land which should yield a gusher. We'll have a derrick and a drill in place there before dawn.'

'And if we're disturbed?' queried Tom Kolb, one of the more thoughtful engineers.

'If we're disturbed, we'll try to parley with the Tribal Council again. We'll dangle the chance of big money to come if they enter into a partnership – on our terms, of course. We'll point out that it's a *fait accompli* – the well is in place and the oil is there, all ready to be brought in.'

'And if they refuse?'

'If they refuse, we'll make a filibustering expedition of it, holding the land by having our gunnies fight for it and setting up our own enclave right there. That's wildcatting, Tom, pure and simple.'

Dix Tynan folded the map and thrust out his blocky chin, looking like Napoleon deciding to invade a new continent.

CHAPTER SIX

ACTION BEYOND THE CREEK

'It strikes me that you two are enjoying this like a couple of schoolboys playing hookey,' opined Slim Oskin. 'I never knew such irresponsibility.'

'There speaks the man who up and walked out on his job as town marshal of Cinch City,' came the ironic reply from Cephas Dannehar. 'Though I have to admit I'm happier in the saddle getting into some kind of action instead of just playing the general and drawing up plans.'

'Hey, calm your enthusiasm for action. We have to remember the Tribal Council wants us to hold back on anything likely to bring problems for the tribe. We're just here to scout around for an eyeful of what is Dragon is up to,' said Abel Aubert. 'And, above all, we mustn't get caught.'

It was night and the trio, having crossed the creek on horseback and riding up from the bottom lands, were now crossing the empty, folded terrain, heading in the direction of the ghost town, Enterprise. There was a slight, warm breeze and, had the three riders not known that the menace of the Dragon Oil Company was crouching in the darkness somewhere ahead of them, they might have called the atmosphere peaceful.

An early quarter moon rode through thin cloud cover, spreading silvery light and, for each of the trio, this riding into land where potential danger lurked brought a tingling thrill from earlier military days when they followed the call of their divided loyalties and ventured through dangerous regions.

Their mission certainly had its reckless schoolboy aspect and the Rapid Creek Tribal Council knew nothing of it but Dannehar, Oskin and Aubert had succumbed to a mutual curiosity. They wanted to know at least a little of the brooding Dragon's strength and possibly what it was planning as it lay inactive in its tumbledown township on the Cherokee settlement's doorstep. Their intention was to scout around the margins of Enterprise and, with luck, even into the town itself to discover what was going on there. It was to be wholly a matter of intelligence-gathering for the company's inaction since the bushwhackings at Rapid Creek surely signified some plan of attack in the brewing. Dragon was not maintaining its camp in this territory without a purpose in mind.

As to risk, their years sat lightly enough upon the three for them to still feel the spirit of their youthful soldiering bright and quick within them. It was the private conviction of each that he was still able to take the chances he once took at places like Chancellorsville, Chickamauga, Gettysburg and Honey Springs and come out with a whole skin.

'Too bad we're hogtied by the Council's wishes,' muttered Cephas Dannehar. 'It's not that I really want trouble but–'

'But if you could set off a few sticks of dynamite under Dragon's new-fangled drilling gear, you would,' finished Oskin drily.

They rode with muffled ringbits, keeping a steady pace, heading for the spot on the horizon where, in daylight, the smudge of drifting smoke marked the position of the derelict town and avoiding anything which looked like a well-marked trail, ever wary of encountering anyone from Enterprise.

Eventually, they hit scrub country, where thick shrubbery grew almost higher than their saddles, giving good cover and the wide expanses of night-shrouded land enfolded ahead of them. Abruptly, they cut a trail where evidence of fairly fresh horse droppings amid wheel-ruts indicated that it was travelled over not too long before. It snaked away into the darkness but it clearly linked the creek and the distant town held by Dragon.

'Keep off the trail,' warned Dannehar. 'No telling who's likely to come along it. Keep to the cover of the scrub, riding alongside the trail and some distance off it.'

This they did, employing all of their old soldiers' caution and plodding steadily ahead without encountering anyone travelling the trail which was fitfully silvered by the moon.

Abel Aubert suddenly caught his breath and strained forward in his saddle.

'Hey, I'm sure I saw a light up ahead!' he said cautiously. 'Just a twinkle and only for a second but I'm sure I saw a light!'

All three riders reined up and held their mounts still while they peered ahead where the trail became lost in the darkness.

'There it goes again!' Aubert said urgently. 'This time I'm sure I saw it.'

'Me too,' confirmed Slim Oskin. 'There's

a light all right and it's coming this way.'

Dannehar swung out of his saddle. 'Better dismount and sit your cayuses down in this high brush and squat until we get some idea of who's on the trail,' he advised. His companions complied, all three swiftly making the best of the concealing brush. From their cover, they saw the light again. Then it became more distinct, growing bigger and swinging from side to side.

'I reckon it's a lantern on a wagon,' reported Oskin. 'There's a wagon heading this way. No – there's more than one!'

There came a mounting sound of rumbling wheels and the tramp of many horses with an accompanying jingle of trappings. The ground began to shudder and vibrate under their advance.

'Sounds like an army on the move,' said Aubert.

The trio crouched deeper into the cover of the brush, yanking their reins to lower their horses' heads. Slithering out of scudding clouds, the moon allowed a brief glimpse of an advancing cavalcade – mounted men accompanying a string of laden wagons, drawing steadily nearer.

'Dragon's heading for the creek,' growled Dannehar.

'They're hauling a heap of gear. Looks like they aim to invade the Cherokee land and you can bet their gang of gunnies are plenty armed,' breathed Slim Oskin.

'We'll have to warn the folks at Rapid Creek pretty quick,' said Aubert anxiously. 'All the guns will have to be rounded up to hold off this bunch.'

The Dragon men were now almost parallel with the spot where the three with their animals were concealed. A squad of outriders, bulky shadows with the outlines of Winchesters slung over their shoulders, came within yards of the trio. At that point, Dannehar's bronc gave a nervous shudder, hoisted its head in defiance of Dannehar's striving to haul it down. The animal loosed a loud, quivering whinny, responding to the presence of the horses on the trail. Immediately, the nearby riders stiffened and one abruptly stood up in his stirrups.

'You damnfool cayuse!' hissed Dannehar through gritted teeth. 'This is the last thing we want!'

'Hey!' croaked the standing horseman breathlessly. 'There's someone out there in the brush!'

There was a sudden surge of action behind him as the silhouettes of horses and weapon-flourishing riders bulked out of the darkness. They came charging ahead in the general direction of the concealed men and horses. A gun barked and a wild, wide shot went screeching through the air.

'Mount up and ride out!' hissed Dannehar.

'Make for the creek! We can't fight this bunch here, there are too many of 'em!'

It meant revealing themselves and risking the fire of the oncoming riders, but all three rose swiftly, dragged their horses to their feet and mounted. They turned the rumps of their animals to the pursuers, who now seemed to be only yards behind, and spurred madly towards the creek. Another shot *zipped* dangerously close to Dannehar's hat. With heads held low against the flying manes of their horses, the trio split the wind across the scrubland, each man instinctively drawing his sixgun as he managed his reins with one hand.

Dannehar turned to Oskin, thundering along neck-and-neck with him.

'Blast you, Slim!' he shouted. 'You got us tangled in a hell of a mess with your harebrained notion of peeking around Dragon's camp!'

'*Me?*' hooted Oskin indignantly. 'It was

your damnfool idea from the start. *You* sold Abel and me on crossing to this side of the creek like a kid planning to play hookey!'

All three spurred their animals yet more vigorously as another shot blasted behind them. Only the darkness of the night and the movement of their mounts was impairing the accuracy of the pursuers' fire. Another display of moonlight would play against the escaping trio.

Dix Tynan, riding at the head of the Dragon column, spluttered in indignation and thumped the arm of Reese whose ungainly frame was saddled beside him.

'What the hell ails your bunch?' he roared. 'They're hollering and shooting fit to wake the dead. Their racket will carry for miles and we're supposed to be sneaking in on the Cherokee. This ruckus will ruin everything. Take after them with some of these other men and shut them up. Bring them back here. They've probably been spooked by some camping saddle-tramps or some such.'

Reese waved to a knot of his henchmen which included the smart-alecky kid who so much irked Dix Tynan. They jogged their horses off the trail and thumped off into the night-shrouded scrub in the dust-swirled wake of the pursuing group. Further sporadic gunfire came echoing back to them from the confused action ahead.

Up at the front of the chase, Dannehar, Oskin and Aubert were streaking ahead, lying flat along their horses' backs and taking care to remain close to each other. None of the wild shots had hit them but the pursuers were coming hard and it could only be a matter of time before one or the other stopped a shot.

They were now impelled by self-preservation and, with a fine disregard for the Tribal Council's desire to avoid starting trouble in the unassigned lands beyond the Rapid Creek settlement, they triggered back an occasional unaimed pistol shot.

'Make for the creek bottom. We can dismount below its rim and fire back from a fixed position,' gasped Dannehar.

Already, the pursuing party was unravelling in the confusion of the darkness with some riders blundering off into the scrub, frustrated through not having clear sight of the pursued. But a tenacious bunch, including the mouthy kid, were clinging to the dust of the trio's backtrail.

Darkness was becoming more intense as the fleeing trio reached the lip of the declivity below which lay the sandy and muddy spread of the creek bottom. The sound of the swiftly running water guided them rather than the sight of the creek and Dannehar was spurred to act by memories of his old role in the Confederate cavalry. With horses and riders almost on the point of plunging down to the creek bottom, he yelled, 'Unsaddle and get down under the rim with our horses!'

All three reined their mounts to an abrupt halt, swung out of their saddles and ran, reins in hand, urging their animals over the edge of the lip, even as several pistols blasted out of the darkness behind them. Under cover of the rim of land, they desperately forced their animals to sit then gave their attention to answering their pursuers' fire, like soldiers shooting over the edge of a trench.

In the darkness of the land above them, there was confusion among the Dragon men. Dannehar, Oskin and Aubert could hear the harsh voice of Dix Tynan bellowing orders against a scrambling of hoofs punctuated by occasional wild firing which sent random shots screaming over the heads of the men and animals, now well concealed below the lip of land.

However, it could only be a matter of time

before their shots allowed the pursuers to pinpoint their position and so enable them to eventually bring all their force against them.

With a mounting pounding of hoofs, a rider came charging blindly out of the blackness to the edge of the rim. There followed an urgent slithering as he tried to halt his horse on realizing that a drop to the creek bottom lay before him. With a gurgling gasp, the rider, who was the mouthy kid so disliked by Tynan, was unhorsed and sent over the edge of the lip flying through the air with flailing arms, to land in the sand and mud scarcely a yard from Dannehar, Oskin and Aubert.

The youngster landed in a heap close to the edge of the swift flow of Rapid Creek. In the course of his fall, he had lost the sixgun he had flourished during the pursuit along with his hat. He sprawled, winded, for a few seconds before he found himself grabbed by Cephas Dannehar and hauled to a sitting position.

The mouth of Dannehar's Colt was thrust into his ribs and Dannehar pushed his face close to that of the captive to ascertain his features. A volley of wild shots came out of the darkness above the lip of the declivity and were speedily answered by Oskin and Aubert, crouching under its shelter.

Above the racket, Dannehar gave a surprised yell. 'Hey, Slim, just look at who's dropped in on us, none other than Mr Cal Stebbins, who was once your guest in the Cinch City gaol!'

CHAPTER SEVEN

BATTLE

The gasping, bewildered youngster, focused his eyes in the darkness and glared at the face of the man who had grabbed him and was prodding his middle with a Colt revolver.

'Cephas Dannehar!' he spluttered. 'You're that damned Cephas Dannehar who beaned me in Cinch City!'

'You bet I am and I'm all set to bean you again if I get half a chance,' confirmed Dannehar. Even as he spoke, with the racket of gunfire as a background to his thought process, he was considering what the discovery of Stebbins in this situation indicated. Clearly, his earlier presence in Cinch City meant he was, like the pair who tried to bushwhack Dannehar and the men encountered in Gunstock, yet another recruit on the way to take Dragon's gunwages. But, puzzlingly, he had made rapid progress to have reached the oil company's camp and be already assimilated into the Dragon crew. Curiously, Dannehar and Oskin had not encountered him on the trail or in Gunstock, the stopping-off place for other Dragon recruits.

'You got yourself up here damned quick since I left you lying on the floor of the hoosegow down in Texas. How the hell did you do it?' growled Dannehar.

Though at a disadvantage, the kid was recovering his brash arrogance. He gave a disdainful grunt. 'By means you used-up oldsters never even thought of,' he sneered. 'You don't know nothing but horseback travel. Bet you never even heard of the railroad. Bet you never even knew there's a line from Denison, Texas, right up to Wagoner, here in Indian Territory. That blasted deputy in Cinch City turned me loose – too plumb raw to even hold me on a gaol-break charge, I guess. I had money in my poke and a cayuse in the livery...'

'...so you rode over to Denison and took a ticket for yourself and your horse to Wagoner. Sure, we know about the railroad link all right, but riding up this way gave us a chance to meet some of the other gents who were recruited by Mr Reese, as I guess you were.'

Behind Dannehar and Stebbins, the fire from the men in the darkness above the rim of the creek bottom was growing more intense. Abel Aubert was shooting back at an enemy he could not see and Slim Oskin was squatting in the lee of the lip, filling the chambers of his Colt from the loops of his shellbelt.

'Dammit! Get over here quick, Cephas, we're running low on ammunition!' he bawled.

'In a second,' answered Dannehar. 'I want to know more from this joker, before I dose him with lead.'

Cal Stebbins' arrogance began to waver. 'You ain't going to kill me in cold blood?' he jittered.

Dannehar prodded him with his pistol again. 'What's this move of Dragon's? A full-scale invasion of the Rapid Creek settlement, I suppose.'

'Yeah, to establish a camp and drill for oil whether the Cherokee like it or not,' said Stebbins in a quivering voice, feeling another forceful jab of the pistol.

In the murkiness behind the pair, Oskin was shooting into the turmoil above the creek bed, his aim guided by the muzzle-flashes from the weapons of the Dragon men while Abel Aubert, with an exhausted sixgun, was rolling over to reach the Winchester in the saddle scabbard of his crouching horse.

'C'mon, Cephas!' he roared as he worked the pump action of the rifle. 'We need you!'

Cal Stebbins received another hard jab from Dannehar's pistol. 'Who's this Reese jasper?' demanded Dannehar. 'We hear he has another name. Who is he really? C'mon, answer before I gut-shoot you!'

The kid was quaking now. 'There's a story saying he's really Tod Heckler,' shuddered the youngster. 'Dammit, Mr Dannehar, you don't really aim to gut-shoot me, do you.'

'Hear that, Slim?' shouted Dannehar into the gun-noisy darkness behind him. 'Remember Tod Heckler?'

'By the great horned toad, I ought to,' roared Oskin with a note of surprise. 'Heckler, the great gunfighter turned bank-robber! I led the posse that grabbed him when I was town marshal in Vermillion Gap, New Mexico. I got him a long stretch in Leavenworth. He swore he'd kill me one day. For the love of Pete, get rid of that fool kid and come back into the fight before we're swamped by this gang!'

'I'll get rid of him, all right,' stated Dannehar icily, prodding Stebbins yet again.

Stebbins gurgled and managed to splutter a pleading, 'Mr Dannehar – you ain't–' His pleading ended in a surprised gurgle as Cephas Dannehar showed him how much of a 'used-up oldster' he was by a display of surprising strength, hauling the youngster to his feet and shoving him through the darkness towards the sound of the swift current of the creek.

'Can you swim, kid?' he growled. The pair were now near the water's edge.

'Yes,' the kid managed to gasp.

'Glad to hear it. Go find some fishes to converse with!'

He gave Stebbins a forceful push in the direction of the noisy water and heard his howl of protest die in the louder sound of a satisfying splash. 'There. You can count yourself a lucky *hombre*. Getting wet is a damn sight better than being gut-shot!' observed Dannehar.

Dannehar scrambled back in the direction of the lip of the creek bottom where there now seemed to be a lull in the firing. Something was happening on the dark plain above them. The intensity of Dragon's fire had lessened, giving the suggestion that the oil company's forces were reforming from their initial scattered positions. Quite likely, they would eventually retaliate with a better thought-out attack on those who were carrying on their form of trench-warfare from the rim of the creek bottom. And they doubtless had superior manpower enough to mount a powerful onslaught.

Reaching the dark form of his squatting animal, Dannehar snatched his Winchester from its scabbard and hunkered down between the horse and Aubert. He laid the rifle in reserve beside him and began to replenish the chambers of his Colt from his belt-loops. He took advantage of the lull to say to Aubert, 'Listen, Abel. We're in a hell of a fix here, so is the whole settlement if this bunch get across the creek. We can't make a sudden break for it, the noise would alert the Dragon gang. Walk your cayuse back along the creek while you've a chance. Mount up when you're clear of this spot and ride like hell, cross the creek and warn Fox and the rest of the young fellows to saddle up and come in smoking.'

'What? And leave you two here to fight it out!' hooted Abel Aubert indignantly. 'And why me, anyway?'

Danneher ducked instinctively as someone out in the darkness loosed a wild shot.

'Because you know the creek and the safest places to ford it in the dark,' he told the schoolteacher. 'And you carry some weight in the community. You know how the Tribal Council feels about involvement in trouble off Cherokee territory.'

'I still don't like leaving you here,' objected Aubert. 'The racket of this fight will alert the men back at the settlement to it anyway.'

'And the Council elders will probably try to hold them back from a ruckus on this side of the creek,' declared Dannehar. 'Their land is under attack, no matter what niceties the Council raise. And, remember, we were attacked first on public land so Federal law is on our side and that of anyone who aids us. Dammit, Abel, you'll have to persuade them back at the settlement that the Dragon outfit must be held back from the Cherokee land.'

'Since you put it that way, I'll go,' growled Aubert. 'Blast it, I was beginning to relish this fix. It was almost like you and me at Honey Springs all over again.'

'Except that both sides were more evenly matched. And you were young and wild then. Now, you're married with social responsibilities,' Dannehar said. 'Keep your head down and ride the creek bottom like all hell.'

Abel Aubert placed his Winchester on the ground. 'An extra gun to help out,' he said. Then he yanked the reins of his horse to bring the animal to a standing position, mounted quickly and disappeared into the darkness, riding below the rim of the declivity.

Up on the land above the rim, all was eerily quiet. Working swiftly in the blackness, Dannehar and Oskin rolled over to lie on their backs and begin replenishing the chambers of their handguns from their diminishing stocks of ammunition.

The lull in the shooting became a total cessation and, from above the rim of the creek bed, there echoed hoarse voices and noises indicative of the movement of wagons and horses.

Gingerly, Slim Oskin rose and looked over the lip of the declivity. Darkness enveloped the vast plain but there was distant activity, discernable by swinging lanterns and the far voices. In the immediate vicinity, there was no evidence of the Dragon men who had pursued the trio this far, suggesting that they had returned to the wagons, probably without realizing anything of Stebbins' mishap in the darkness.

'Looks like they're gathering themselves together,' reported Oskin. 'Could be we have a tolerable chance to sneak out of here.'

'Nothing doing,' responded Dannehar who, working by touch in the dark, was checking the ammunition in his own Winchester and in the one left by Abel Aubert. 'They were marching toward this portion of the creek, which means they know there's a good crossing point for their wagons somewhere here and I figure they'll surely continue. We'll have to lie low here and hold them back as best we can, hoping Abel can whip up a defensive force to keep them from crossing.'

'Doggone, you sure never change much,' grumbled Oskin. 'Crossing the creek on a crackpot notion; achieving nothing but becoming holed up in the face of an enemy force of unknown strength and persisting in holding out. It's no wonder your side lost the big war. And you'd the all-fired gall to blame it all on me to boot. I should have stayed in Cinch City where I was nicely settled.'

Dannehar allowed himself a mischievous grin. Ribbing Oskin when they were in a tight corner was a pleasure he'd enjoyed since their first days on the trail.

'If you'd stayed in Cinch City, you'd have got so darned fat and respectable and settled they'd probably have made you mayor,' countered Dannehar. 'You can thank me for happening along to break the monotony and revitalize your life.'

'And, to return to my original complaint, for getting me in this hole,' muttered Oskin. He suddenly became alert and peered over the lip of the declivity and into the darkness. 'Hear that, Cephas?' he said. 'That Dragon bunch is definitely moving this way. We'll have a hell of a job holding them back, just you and me.'

'We call stall 'em by using bluff,' stated Dannehar coolly.

'Bluff?' spluttered Oskin. 'What kind of bluff can two play against a crew who're armed to the teeth?'

Dannehar sighed wearily. 'That remark just shows how blamed settled and soft-brained you've become through living the easy life in Cinch City,' he retorted. 'Have you forgotten the old shoot and roll trick?'

Slim Oskin gave a slow-dawning grin, like one in whose brain a great light was becoming visible. 'The old shoot and roll trick!' he breathed. 'It might just work – for a while at least.'

CHAPTER EIGHT

RIDERS IN THE NIGHT

Abel Aubert urged his tired horse over the uncertain terrain of the dark-shrouded creek bottom, moving urgently but with caution.

To his left lay the ribbon of Rapid Creek, unseen in the darkness but making its presence known by the constant sound of its rushing current. Beyond the creek was the settlement of the Cherokee where Aubert knew he could muster the assistance of the young men who had long stood ready to resist the menace which they knew must eventually come from a fuller encroachment by Dragon.

Aubert knew the creek bottom fairly well but from the opposite side of the water. He was now on unassigned land on which he had rarely travelled before, whereas he had an understanding of the geography of the settlement side. He knew there were safe crossing places but he was so handicapped by the night and ignorant of the terrain that seeking reliable guiding landmarks was difficult. In the darkness, he was not at all sure even of the point where he had crossed with Dannehar and Oskin, but he reasoned it could not be far from where he and his companions had finally holed up. After all, the Dragon crew were making in that general direction and they must have earlier scouted the land for a crossing point for their invasion of the Indian lands.

As he rode, a fury of anxious thoughts surged through the brain of Rapid Creek's schoolmaster. The people who had adopted his family and himself had experienced trouble enough from Dragon and it was now evident that the oilmen were bent on depredations on a bigger scale.

Every fibre of Aubert's being ached to do something decisive to halt the threat to the Indian settlement which had become his home and wherein he had a powerful emotional stake. He was fortunate enough to be born a free man in territory where slavery was not enforced but was the subject of often murderous turmoil. He had lived in Kansas through the years when it became 'Bloody Kansas' and where its own private war raged a decade before the whole nation split into full-scale civil war.

When that bloodthirsty day arrived and the Union raised regiments from among the black freemen, he was an early recruit to the First Kansas Coloured Infantry. His natural instincts were peaceful and scholarly but his zeal for the Union cause made him a good soldier and the three stripes which eventually graced his sleeves were well earned.

Aubert distinguished himself in many battles before he was pitched into what was almost a sideshow to the war, the engagement at Honey Springs out in the west, far from the major clashes between the armies of Abraham Lincoln and Jefferson Davis. He came out of that sharp, rain-sodden affair with a shattered leg and, when found by the Cherokee, half-conscious and left on the field, his emotional tie to that people was secured. They sheltered him, nursed him and eventually assisted him to find his way back to the Union position. He was lame and knew he was probably of no further use to the army, but he would not turn quitter. He would not leave the army until officially discharged. Even then, he argued with his superiors that he might still fill an army desk job. All to no avail.

Back in Kansas, life was no easier than before the war, but at least he had his young wife and he made a modest living as a clerk for a sympathetic merchant. With the defeat of the south, and the dawning of the bitter period called Reconstruction, Kansas and the neighbouring region was as scarred by brutality as before the war. Now, savage gangs of former Confederate guerrillas turned outlaw ranged the countryside and then came the Ku Klux Klan, the masked riders who aimed to wreak savage vengence in the name of the southern dead. Black men and women were their prime targets.

Aubert's thoughts turned to the raw lands of the west where he was treated so well in the Cherokee Nation. A man such as himself might make a new start there and find the opportunity and contentment for his family which was denied them in the region called the Middle Border, which was still virtually at war.

He and his wife packed, took the road west and were welcomed by the old friends at the Rapid Creek settlement. Among them, Aubert and Marietta found their measure of happiness – and of heartbreak through the death of their young child – and he repaid his old debt of gratitude by his contribution as schoolteacher to the Cherokee youngsters.

Riding the margin of the creek through the darkness, he reflected that what he and his family found at Rapid Creek and helped to further had already been savaged by the dark-of-the-moon depredations of Dragon, and now it was threatened by something of an even larger scale. The people and their settlement were worth defending to the very death and he made a savage vow that he was prepared to do just that.

All the time, he was conscious that Dannehar and Oskin faced danger from the weighty forces of Dragon back at their isolated spot and it was essential that he brought help. He was becoming increasingly frustrated at his inability to locate a crossing place while the rushing of the water seemed to be a mocking voice.

Then, it was overridden by another sound, that of mounting hoofbeats, thundering along the creek bottom towards him. Now, the first thin silver and gold streaks of dawn were appearing in the sky. Aubert squinted ahead and saw them coming: a mass of riders, heading for him directly and purposefully and he was full in their path.

'Hell!' he spat. 'Dragon men! A bunch of them have worked around me and come off the plain down to the creek bottom to head me off! OK, if a defence to the death is called for, that's the way it'll have to be!'

He spurred his mount ahead toward the horsemen, at the same time speedily hauling his sixgun from its leather.

Once again, Dix Tynan's ire had risen to boiling point. He was trying to hasten his wildcat crew along the trail to make a crossing of the creek while darkness remained, but the incident which sent a set of his men in pursuit of whoever made their presence felt in the darkness was an unwanted interruption of the plan in hand.

There had been some confused shooting and yelling and beating of hoofs but Tynan had no idea of what transpired out yonder. Now, the riders were straggling back to the main body of the Dragon party. So far as the night allowed him to see anything, Tynan could observe that they were dejected and frustrated. The first recognizable figure he saw was that of the gunman who called himself Reese, slumped in his saddle.

'What in hell was going on out there, Reese?' Tynan bellowed. 'Who were those jokers? What were they up to?'

'Darned if I know. There seemed to be at least three guys but I figure we hazed 'em off,' growled Reese. 'Yep, we sure hazed 'em off all right.' He tagged on the addition to give the impression of some positive achievement, then added further, 'But we lost the kid. He just disappeared.'

'The kid? That youngster with all the talk? Hell, if they killed him and his body is lying out in the brush it'll be damned incriminating if it's discovered,' shouted Tynan. 'We don't want Dragon's dead littering either the unassigned land or the land of the Nations. We've no right to be on either, remember?'

It seemed to Reese that the Dragon boss was wholly blaming him for this hitch in his progress toward invading Rapid Creek. 'Damn it, there was nothing I could about it,' he hooted indignantly. 'He was with us one minute, then, in all the ruckus, he just plumb vanished.'

'Blast it. You and some of the others had better hang around here and search for him,' stipulated Dix Tynan. 'Before we know it, it'll be dawn and we'll lose the advantage of surprise. If you find the kid's corpse, make sure you bury him well – and don't leave any traces.'

Tynan turned his attention to the gathering of wagons, horses and men which, up to this point, had been moving slowly but was now stalled while the field boss gave his attention to Reese and the horsemen just returned from the chase.

'C'mon!' he yelled angrily. 'Keep moving! Quit wasting time standing around!'

At that moment, a shot blasted out from somewhere close to the creek bottom and a bullet *whanged* through the space between Dix Tynan and the mounted Reese. The shot travelled upward as though it was fired from a position close to the earth. Instinctively, Tynan dropped to the ground for cover and Reese and the other mounted men close to him quickly left their saddles and hunkered low. A second shot barked and a bullet screamed close enough to a horse in the trail crew to make it whinny in fear.

Dix Tynan, sprawling on the ground, tried to pierce the darkness out where the shots were coming from and yet another muzzle-flame and screeching shot blasted forth, bringing an anguished yell from among the trail crew, 'Hell! I'm hit! It got me in the arm!'

Tynan saw another white flash from some distance to the left of the last one, then yet another from further to the right. All the shots were coming from low positions along the rim beyond which lay the creek bottom, as if a line of sharpshooters was spaced out through the brush, pegging random shots towards the Dragon crew.

'There's a whole damn crew of 'em out there,' hooted Dix, who had now assumed that the opposition was from a force from the Rapid Creek settlement which had crossed the creek. He issued urgent instructions to the men on the trail. 'Bunch up, you men. Shoot back and keep the horses from panicking!'

He hauled out his revolver and began to trigger shots randomly towards the direction of the hostile fire.

Out there, along the rim of the creek bottom, Cephas Dannehar and Slim Oskin were operating their old shoot-and-roll game with considerable glee, although they knew it was a game which could quickly be played out, leaving them in as vulnerable a position as before.

The pair had inched their way up from the creek bottom, bringing their Winchesters as well as the one left by Abel Aubert as a spare. They lay side by side in the brush, each levelling his rifle and the spare weapon was laid between them.

'Six shots as we roll out and six coming back. The spare is a standby in case we wind up in a real hole,' stipulated Dannehar. 'Let's go.'

So their old device of rolling and shooting was put into action. Dannehar made a complete roll to the right while Oskin did the same to the left. Each fired a shot, then rolled rapidly further to the left and right and fired again.

In the darkness, with the snipers unsighted by their opponents, it appeared that the shots were coming from a number of riflemen positioned along the rim of the creek bottom. It was an illusion which took the Dragon crew totally by surprise and the first qualms of panic were appearing among them, particularly as one of the crew had been hit by a random shot.

'How many are out there?' squawked a jittery voice. 'Seems like there's a whole bunch of 'em, lying out in a line in front of us.'

'Bunch up! Get under the wagons and keep shooting back!' bellowed Dix Tynan. 'It'll soon be dawn and we'll be able to see 'em.' He fired a couple of hopeful shots out into the darkness.

Their unseen assailants were now engaged

in the second part of the illusion, each having completed his half-dozen rolls interspersed by shots. Now they were rolling back to the position where they had left the spare Winchester and following the same pattern of shooting between each roll. They came together, each grinning with satisfaction.

'Take the spare while I reload, Slim,' said Dannehar. 'Give 'em a shot now and again but keep shifting around the brush. Don't let that bunch pin you to any one position. They must have enough fire power to finish us off – if they get their wits together long enough to use it.' He began to push loose shells from a supply in the pocket of his jeans into the magazine of his Winchester. 'I reckon we've stalled their move for a while and scared 'em pretty good.'

In no case was that more true than in that of the swaggering roughneck known as Reese.

The truth about Reese was not only that he was really Tod Heckler, broken down gunfighter and thwarted bank robber, but also he was pretty close to being totally washed up – and he knew it.

His swagger was merely a front. His stretch in the penitentiary, where he was lodged through the diligence of Marshal Slim Oskin, had taken much of the real fight out him. Times had changed while he was behind bars and the west was changing too. The ethos was rapidly becoming less and less that which bred the likes of Tod Heckler and, for that matter, the likes of Cephas Dannehar and Slim Oskin, too. He had been released into a world where many of the old-time desperados were in their graves or in discreet retirement and where stock companies had taken over from the feisty independent ranchers who were happy to have trigger-trippers on their payrolls for the protection of their outfits. He'd grown paunchy in jail for the grub had not been too bad and he'd endured much idleness. He was hardly a fearsome figure any more.

The best he could do was find himself a place with an outfit such as Dragon where he could talk big and draw easy money.

Now, he had the ghastly feeling that it was all about to unravel.

Crouching beside his horse, ducking the zinging bullets from the gunmen in the darkness, he figured he'd had enough. He had enough of Dix Tynan's tough attitude and harsh tongue. Taking Dragon's wages was all very well, but why the hell should he risk being killed out here on the plains of

Indian Territory to help men living in mansions in the east to enjoy even softer lives?

More drastic among the fears which were beginning to grip him with icy fingers was one concerning those who had appeared out of the darkness to open fire on the Dragon wildcatting team. Suppose they were the forces of law and order which, out in this country of Indian settlements and hole-in-the-wall white men's towns, was loosely-knit, scattered and in the hands of a variety of agencies but which nevertheless existed? The most powerful was that operated by Federal Judge Isaac C Parker, from his base at Fort Smith, over in Arkansas.

Judge Parker's judgements – and his gallows – had a reputation which caused shudderings among badmen across the west and his Federal Marshals were known for their leech-like tenacity when it came to tracking down offenders.

The man known to the Dragon company as Reese was not all big talk. He had initiated and led brutal and cowardly depredations against the Indians of Rapid Creek to further Dragon's ambitions of reaching the lake of oil which the company believed lay under the settlement. There were the bushwhacking and farm burning incidents which could

167

put him on the gallows at Fort Smith and, crouching with his horse under the beginning streaks of dawn as what appeared to be a line of riflemen put the Dragon crew under a determined attack, Reese gave in to his yellow streak. In a cold sweat, he decided he'd quit Dragon then and there, while he still had a whole neck and while it was still dark enough to make a bolt for it unseen by the Dragon wildcatters, who were now clustered around and under their wagon answering the fire of their attackers.

They were far too occupied to notice Reese, alias Tod Heckler, trying to hug the ground to make himself as inconspicuous as possible, leading his horse off into the darkness of the brush behind the position of the Dragon wagons and sneaking away well out of range of the bullets of the assailants.

He was hitting the trail, pronto. He did not know where he would finish but he was making sure it was not going to be on Judge Parker's gallows.

He led his horse through the brush, moving as swiftly as he could to distance himself from where the Dragon trail crew had now formed itself into a defensive knot around its wagons with its members shooting wildly in the direction of the creek.

Once he was good and clear of the action, he would mount up and ride. Westward was surely the best way to travel so he could shake the dust of this damned Indian Territory from his boots, he reasoned.

Reese had no clear idea of a destination, but thought he might rest up for a spell in one of the hole-in-wall outlaw towns towards the Red River, then cross into Texas. A man could lose himself in Texas. He was travelling light, without any saddlebags, blankets or trail-gear but, at least, he still had a fairly full poke of Dragon's wages, even after his extravagances in Arrow Flat.

He thought bitterly that he sure wouldn't miss any part of the Dragon enterprise except the wages. He'd earned them all right but, in doing so, he'd also earned himself the dire prospect of a Fort Smith rope around his neck.

When the sounds of battle were well behind him and with dawn widening in the sky, he climbed into the saddle and set his horse's nose to the west.

'Move, cayuse,' he growled. 'Let's get the hell out of here.'

Back at the Dragon crew, Dix Tynan was holed up behind the wheel of a wagon carrying drilling gear, thumbing bullets into the chambers of a sixgun he had just been discharging with badly aimed abandon towards whoever had his crew under attack. Around him, the Dragon men were sprawled on the ground or sheltering under the wagons, blasting shots in the direction of the creek with anything but military precision.

Tynan was in a state of high indignation, interspersing hoarsely shouted orders with swearing of a blistering quality. 'It must be them damned Indians from over the creek,' he spat. He looked up to take in the spreading light of dawn. 'Dammit, we might have made a start if we'd crossed while it was dark. Somehow, they've caught us flat-footed.'

Out in the brush, Dannehar and Oskin had come together again and were acutely aware that, under the spreading light of the dawn, their position and their puny strength could be more easily spotted by the enemy. The roll-and-fire trick had confused the Dragon crew for a while under the cover of darkness but it would now become clear that there was not a strong force of riflemen lined up in the path of the trail crew.

Furthermore, they were now critically short of ammunition. They had three rifles and their handguns, but the wild nature of the exchange of shots meant that much lead had been spent in merely shooting at random without having much effect on the Dragon crew apart from halting progress towards the creek. Now, they were highly vulnerable. Once the Dragon men fully grasped that they were faced by a mere two men who were constrained by dwindled ammunition, the oilmen could move swiftly against them with deadly force.

The pair were sprawled full-length behind a patch of scrub as a tense lull descended over the land and Dannehar was trying to mentally estimate what amount of ammunition they might have between them. From their position, they could just make out the oilmen, forted up around their wagons.

'Do you figure they know just where we are?' whispered Slim Oskin.

'Maybe not right now, but they'll pretty soon discover us unless they're dumber than I think,' Dannehar replied. 'They've got us nailed down between themselves and the creek.'

'Looks like our only hope is to slither back to the creek bed on our bellies and find our cayuses – if they haven't been scared off by all the racket,' said Oskin. 'You and your blamed shoot-and-roll trick. All you did was get us into a deeper hole than we were in before!'

At that moment, a rifle shot cracked from behind them and a bullet screamed over their heads. Almost at once, the shot was followed by a drumming of horses from the direction of the creek bed.

Cephas Dannehar spat in disgust and suddenly felt the weariness brought on by the long, tense and violent night in which their efforts had, it seemed, proved futile after all.

'All right,' he growled to his companion. 'This time, I'll concede a point to all your bellyaching. A bunch of them have somehow flanked around us in the darkness and are coming up behind us hell for leather. We *are* in a hole, sure enough.'

Then he and Oskin almost shoved their noses into the earth to keep clear of two further angry shots which *whanged* over their heads from the rear.

CHAPTER NINE

DRAGON'S RECKONING

Dannehar and Oskin hugged the ground then rolled over on to their backs, swinging up their Winchesters to deal with the menace thundering at them from the creek bottom at their rear.

They saw a squad of horsemen, lunging forward in their saddles and shooting with Colts and Winchesters over the heads of the pair on the ground, aiming at the Dragon trail crew halted ahead. They caught glimpses of Indian braids and feathers among the oncoming riders and recognized the faces of Fox and others of the Rapid Creek Cherokee settlement. Here and there, strengthening sunlight flashed on the badges of United States Marshals and United States Indian Police.

And riding to the fore, with his white teeth showing in a triumphant grin, was Abel Aubert. He was waving his sixgun in one hand and, with the other, he whipped off his hat and made a cheerful flourish with it towards the men sprawled in the brush.

'Cephas, Slim! Keep your heads down!' he bellowed. 'The Rapid Creek boys and a few friends are coming in smoking as instructed!'

'By cracky!' exploded Slim Oskin, scrambling upward to a crouch and facing the riders, now drawing much closer. 'He's brought a bunch of friends of tolerable good quality. That fellow with the big moustache riding alongside him is Tobe van Epper, one of Judge Parker's chief marshals. You've heard of van Epper, haven't you, Cephas.'

'I'll say I have. He's hauled in some hard cases in his time and hastened plenty into their graves. I'm right glad to see a man with his reputation showing up on my side at a time like this.'

The horsemen came sweeping up from the creek bed behind Dannehar and Oskin with the big moustached United States Marshal, Tobe van Epper, two younger men wearing marshal's badges and Rapid Creek's black schoolteacher in the lead. As they approached they formed themselves into line-abreast like a cavalry unit, making a formidable array of determined Indian faces, feathers and sombreros and with the sun touching a variety of businesslike weaponry.

With foghorn force van Epper hooted a message which carried over the heads of Dannehar and Oskin and along the trail.

'You men ahead! This is a United States posse demanding that you lay down your arms! Resist us and you'll pay dearly!'

As the line continued to advance, Abel Aubert spurred his mount on to meet Dannehar and Oskin who were afoot in the brush. Coming close to them, he swung out of the saddle and limped to meet them, leading his horse.

'Hell, Abel, how did you collect this bunch?' grinned Dannehar. 'It looks like a cavalry division. We figured we'd been outflanked by the Dragon gang when we heard you coming.'

'So did I at first,' laughed Aubert. 'I was down on the creek bottom in the darkness and damned near lost when they came into my path. I was sure Dragon had jumped me and would finish me off pronto. By sheer good luck, the powers that be, including Judge Parker's establishment over at Fort Smith, had set investigations into the lawlessness in the Nations into motion at last. Marshal van Epper and his men, with the help of the Indian Police, were investigating reports of the doings at Rapid Creek. They were there when the racket of the fighting here echoed back.'

'Which, I suppose, caused Fox and his squad to get into action,' supplied Slim Oskin.

'Sure thing. They couldn't saddle up fast enough and Marshal van Epper swore the whole bunch in as deputies,' said Aubert. 'They crossed the creek to investigate the shooting and I rode up into their faces. I had my gun in my fist and was ready to go down fighting. I was plumb lucky I didn't start shooting.'

'Well, by thunder. It looks like the tide has turned against the Dragon bunch!' enthused Dannehar, walloping Aubert heartily on the back. He turned to Oskin and urged, 'C'mon, Slim, these boys are going to make war against that crew yonder and we want to be in on it!'

'Dammit,' howled Oskin. 'We haven't any horses.'

'Hah! Complaining to the last!' scorned Dannehar impatiently. 'We have some ammunition left. We'll just have to join them on foot.'

An hour before the party of riders swept in on Dannehar and Oskin, before the sun was yet risen, Tod Heckler, known as Reese, was making progress through the brush, having put the position of the Dragon trail-crew well behind him. He was intent on moving fast, keeping the creek on his left. He reasoned that, sparing his horse by resting up every couple of hours, he'd make one of the obscure hole-in-the-wall towns, which he knew lay down towards the Red River, somewhere around nightfall. With money in his poke, there he would find accommo-dation, grub and feed for his mount. In a very short time, the Indian Nations would know him no more and he would be well beyond the ken of the Dragon Oil Com-pany.

He permitted himself a dry chuckle. Tod Heckler, he told himself, was no fool. The money paid out by Dragon was good but life was sweet and his fancy was for a life of ease. When all was considered, Dragon's money was not worth a man getting himself killed for.

Then he saw a hunched and miserable figure, trudging along through the brush ahead of him. It was vaguely familiar, dejected and lost looking.

Cautiously, Heckler rode towards the man, placing his hand on the gun butt at his belt. Maybe this was some kind of a trick. One never knew what one was up against with those jaspers who'd run in with the Dragon crew in the darkness.

The figure halted as the horseman approached and, in the widening light of dawn, obviously recognized the rider. He called in a familiar voice, 'Reese? Is that you?'

Tod Heckler grunted in surprise. This was the cocky kid from the Dragon crew, horseless, hatless and decidedly woebegone. Heckler reined his mount.

'What the Sam Hill are you doing here, kid?' he called.

'Quitting, that's what. I've had enough of Dragon and Tynan and this whole damned business. If they've sent you to find me, you can go to hell.'

'I'm quitting, too,' stated Heckler unashamedly. 'None of it is worth a man risking his neck. What happened to you? I figured that bunch we tangled with in the dark finished you off.'

'There was no bunch,' Cal Stebbins responded. 'There were three of 'em. They got me and threw me in the creek. I was swept along by the current and managed to make it to this side and climb out. Lucky thing I wasn't swept on to the Cherokee side of the water. I'm wet all through, lost my gun and horse and I'm damned if I know where I am but I've finished with the Dragon outfit, that's for sure.'

'Only three?' echoed Heckler. 'We chased only three guys back yonder?'

'Yeah and two of 'em were those damned old marshals, Dannehar and Oskin.'

'Oskin!' exploded Heckler. 'You mean Slim Oskin?'

'Sure. He was marshal in Cinch City and he gaoled me. That blasted Dannehar, he—'

But Heckler was not listening to the youngster's grievance against Cephas Dannehar. The very name of Slim Oskin, whose determination and tenacity had landed him in Leavenworth, was poison to Heckler. His yellow streak had been dictating his actions in the last few hours, but the mention of Oskin brought out something from his innards which began to override it: the burning urge to get even with Oskin which had nagged at him for years. He never imagined that Oskin might be right here in the Indian Nations, possibly within reach of the vengeance the broken-down gunman and failed bank robber had dreamed of ever since the judge passed a gaol sentence on him long ago.

Notions began to chase themselves through his thick skull, notions of getting even with Slim Oskin. Something of the savage viciousness he had possessed in younger days was suddenly asserting itself. He might be putting himself up against a tough proposition, particularly when Oskin was sided by the like of Cephas Dannehar but, by thunder, he'd quit running and go in search of Oskin. He wanted a reckoning in bullets – with the final account showing all the profit on his side. He wanted Slim Oskin dead.

'Where are they now, Dannehar and Oskin?' he asked.

'I don't know. Somewhere back along the creek bed where that damned Dannehar threw me in the water, I guess. Listen, Reese, if you're headed back over the Red into Texas, I'll join up with you–'

'Shut up,' growled Heckler. He was thinking hard but his thinking was interrupted by the sounds of shooting far in his backtrail, in the direction of the halted Dragon trailcrew. Something in the way of a fight was still in progress there.

'We can team up,' persisted Cal Stebbins. 'I've got money in my poke and I guess you must have, too. We can pool it. That'll take us a long way–'

'You haven't got a cayuse,' objected Heckler.

'Well, I can get one from somewheree.'

That alerted Heckler's full attention. 'Not in my company, you won't!' he snarled. 'If you steal a horse and we're caught, the pair of us will hang. That's what they do to horse thieves in Indian Territory.'

'Well,' pleaded the kid, 'we could share your horse, taking turns, one riding, one walking. Damn it, you can't leave me out here afoot and without any grub or weapons and soaked to the skin.'

'You'll dry out fast enough when the sun is up,' said Heckler unsympathetically. There was, however, an idea beginning to dawn on him. Perhaps he could use the kid.

The gnawing hatred of Slim Oskin that Heckler had nurtured all these years had now dispelled even the cowardice that made him abandon the Dragon crew during the fight in the night. He sorely wanted to kill Oskin but knew that as a gunfighter he had gone to seed. Furthermore, Oskin had an ally in Dannehar, a man with as formidable a gun reputation as Oskin, and taking on the two of them would be a tall proposition. Not that Heckler intended to settle his grievance in anything like a fair and square manner. He was already formulating vague notions of discovering Oskin's whereabouts, laying for him and shooting him from ambush.

It was an attractive idea but not something he fancied trying alone when Oskin was sided by Cephas Dannehar. Heckler looked down from his saddle at the miserable figure of the kid. He knew Stebbins was brash and mouthy. He did not know if he was any good with a gun but, often enough, he'd displayed a mean streak and he had his own burning grudge against Dannehar. He might make a useful partner in Heckler's murderous scheme.

'Listen, maybe we *can* settle Oskin and Dannehar together. If we combine our brains,' suggested Heckler. 'When the chance arises, I'll get Oskin and you get Dannehar.'

The kid looked at him eagerly. 'What about guns?' he asked. 'I've lost mine.'

'I have a Colt .45 and a Winchester in my saddle scabbard,' said Heckler. 'You take one and I take the other – and I'm taking the rifle.' He stipulated the last bit emphatically. When it came to standing-off odds – or shooting a man from ambush – a powerful pump-action Winchester was far superior to a handgun.

Heckler was offering Cal Stebbins the thin end of the plan and it was even thinner than it appeared to Stebbins because other considerations were working in Heckler's treacherous brain. He had a horse and Stebbins was on foot. He would ensure that he kept control of the animal as well as of the Winchester. If Heckler's plan worked out to his satisfaction, he would quickly abandon his young ally and that was best accomplished in a saddle.

Heckler added some inducement to his proposition. 'We can share the horse, taking turns riding and we can rest him every once in a while.' He did not, of course, reveal his ultimate intention of ensuring that he would be the one who escaped from any tight situation on horseback.

Blinded by the prospect of getting even with Dannehar who had humiliated him in every encounter, Cal Stebbins fell for it. In his lust for vengeance, he failed to see the plan's deficiency in having one participant horseless in country which demanded horses.

'OK,' he said eagerly. 'Give me a chance to ride now. I've been staggering around here in the brush since God knows when.'

Heckler swung down from his mount. The

light of day was strengthening and, from the direction of the halted Dragon trail-crew, there came a crashing of shots.

'Something big going on out that way,' observed Heckler, 'and you say there were only three men in that ruckus we got into. I figure there's a battle starting up yonder, but we ain't getting into it.'

'We sure ain't,' affirmed Cal Stebbins as he mounted the horse then accepted the Colt which Heckler handed up to him. 'We'll have to travel that way, though.'

'We have no choice,' said Heckler. 'But only to locate Dannehar and Oskin and settle with 'em. Dix Tynan, Dragon Oil and the whole boiling of 'em can go to hell.'

And the ill-matched pair, one riding and the other walking, headed back towards the sound of battle, each driven by his own unreasoning hatred and blood-lust.

Dog-tired and bleary eyed, Cephas Dannehar and Slim Oskin carried their Winchesters and trudged along in the banners of dust raised by the squad of Indians and US Marshals, led by Tobe van Epper, like a couple of infantrymen. They were utterly determined to be in on what looked like developing into the last act of a drama.

Oskin spat dust from his mouth. 'A fine situation!' he grumbled. 'Everyone else riding and us without horses – and I figure we don't have much ammunition left. Blast it, Cephas, we came here to help out the Rapid Creek people and now we've got the Cherokee into exactly the situation the Tribal Council didn't want. They're on this side of the creek, out of their own nation and on unassigned land.'

'And upholding United States law,' countered Dannehar. 'You heard van Epper say they've all been properly sworn as deputies. I declare, Slim, if you woke up and found yourself in heaven, you'd still gripe. Duck your head, there's some hot lead around!'

Sporadic shooting was coming from the Dragon party on the trail and the mounted men, now closing in on the collection of horses and wagons were answering.

Tobe van Epper hooted forth another command, 'You men, yonder, put up your guns! Continue shooting and you'll be smoked out pretty damned quick!'

In the Dragon party, Dix Tynan saw support wavering. For all the use he was, the man known as Reese who was taken on to ramrod the mixed bunch of idlers and broken-down gunsharps, supposedly to

185

provide the exploration crew's security, had deserted. His leadership was always dubious but now the trail crew was deprived of even that. Several were ceasing their half-hearted attempts to hold off the mounted men who were rapidly advancing.

Dragon's hired gunhands were sheltering under wagons or behind the heaps of engineering equipment stacked on them, while the pugnacious Tynan, sixgun in hand, moved among them, bent almost double as bullets *zinged* from the speedily advancing horsemen. 'Keep on shooting!' he roared. 'Hell, we've come this far and the company has thousands of dollars at stake here.'

An appeal for loyalty to the company had no effect on most of the men and Dragon's engineers who were not notably belligerent in the first place, were quivering in their boots.

'To hell with the company, that's Uncle Sam's law yonder and I don't want to go inside a federal pen,' jittered one man. He threw down his gun, slithered out from behind a sheltering wagon wheel and lit out on foot in the lee of the Dragon wagons.

'Nor me,' said another, crouching beside his kneeling horse. 'It's Judge Parker's law and I'm keeping clear of Parker's court.' He hauled the animal to its feet, mounted and sped away in the wake of the running man.

The attacking horsemen were halting within easy range of the Dragon crew, sending discouraging shots over the tops of the wagons and heads of the men and the panic was spreading among the wildcatters.

'Better quit resisting!' shouted Tobe van Epper. 'We've got you flat-footed. Your game is finished and you know it.'

A couple of badly aimed shots, fired out of bravado, burst from the wagons, but the morale of the men was shattered.

Dannehar and Oskin trudged through swirling gunsmoke and dust into the midst of the assortment of marshals, Indians and policemen.

'By cracky, they're giving up,' panted Slim Oskin. 'They're coming out of cover like scared rabbits.'

Dix Tynan and the other Dragon men were walking dispiritedly forward to be met by van Epper, the Fort Smith marshals and Indian policemen.

'You fellers did a plumb solid job, holding these jokers on the trail the way you did till we arrived,' one marshal told Dannehar and Oskin as he passed them, flourishing a pair of handcuffs. 'Right good strategy.'

187

'There you are. Right good strategy, and all on account of my generalship,' smirked Dannehar.

'Generalship nothing!' exploded Oskin. 'You brought Abel and me out here on a crackpot whim and got us into a hole – and you know it!'

Abel Aubert came riding up, accompanied by two young Cherokee horsemen from Rapid Creek. They were leading two familiar saddle-horses.

'These boys were guarding the backtrail by the creek bottom and they found your horses grazing happily down there,' he announced.

'Well, they're a welcome sight,' declared Oskin. 'I'm sick of walking. I figure I'm raising a crop of corns already.'

'What do you reckon will happen to these oil jokers?' asked Dannehar.

'Well, on the way here, Tobe van Epper said he aimed to herd 'em all to the nearest gaol which is up in Muskogee and hold 'em for investigations. Seems they're breaking a whole slew of laws just by being here, prospecting for oil and for contemplating encroaching on the lands of the Cherokee Nation,' said Aubert. 'Then there's matter of the burning and killing that went on over at Rapid Creek. The Sooners are choirboys compared to this bunch. After all, most Sooners just want to grab a section of land and raise a crop and a family.'

Tobe van Epper came riding up, a broad grin spreading under his huge moustache. 'I reckon that was a pretty good start to the day,' he rumbled. 'They can't beat us old timers when it comes to badge-toting.'

'Most of the talk I hear is that our kind are pretty well being cancelled out,' said Dannehar.

'Don't believe it,' said van Epper. 'Plenty of lawmen will be needed if future plans are going to work out right. Changes are coming. That's why we've been told to strengthen activities in Indian Territory and Oklahoma Territory. There's even a chance of full statehood in a few years.' He took out a corncob pipe and began to fill it. 'Whispers from higher authority are that Washington aims to section out this region pretty soon and open it to homesteaders and farmers. So, that means clearing out the outlaws, the horse-thieves, the liquor-runners and the Sooners who try to grab the land without permission – and the damned wildcatters who're crazy about this oil stuff.'

The US Marshal got his pipe going

satisfactorily and said through a cloud of smoke, 'We've been instructed to range through this country in some force ahead of all the changes that're bound to come.'

'That's plumb comforting to know,' said Danneher. 'It looked like the Cherokee at Rapid Creek had been forgotten by the authorities.'

'Not so. Word of the doings around here has been seeping through. It's just that we've been short of officers. For a long time, we've heard about the kind of ranahan that's been drifting into this region and we knew about Dragon encroaching on unassigned land. By the way, an Indian policeman down near the Red River found the graves of the two jokers you planted and your note and reported back. We figured that if the celebrated Dannehar and Oskin were butting in, it was time for those who're rightly in charge to be more involved. Judge Parker over at Fort Smith believed your note and figured you truly killed 'em in self-defence. It seems they had bad reputations elsewhere. There'll be no charges against you. Same with the shooting scrap in Gunstock, which we also investigated. All the virtue was on your side, it seems.'

Abel Aubert chuckled, 'You boys need a

rest and so do I. I figure the people back at Rapid Creek are in a mood to give you a right royal welcome. I suggest we leave Marshal van Epper and his friends to their duties here while we head back to some comfort.'

'And maybe to Marietta's cooking,' said Slim Oskin hopefully.

CHAPTER TEN

TWO FOR THE TRAIL

Cal Stebbins was beginning to become dispirited all over again. He was also wearied by the exertions of the night as well as by his experience in the swift and buffeting waters of Rapid Creek, although his clothing was now almost dry. Coming upon Tod Heckler, whom he still knew as Reese, had seemed to offer some respite from his woes. The flabby ex-gunfighter had at least handed him a weapon and, even though sharing a horse, which was about as weary as both Heckler and the kid, was not ideal, it was better than trudging afoot in riding boots the whole time.

Stebbins had no idea of the treachery at Heckler's core, that Heckler would merely use him while he needed an ally then quickly dispose of him – even by killing him.

The pair were making a slow way back in the direction of Dragon's halted trail-crew but with no intention of going there. There had been furious indications from up that way that something spectacular had taken place, but the sounds of battle which had sent flattened echoes over the wide land had now ceased. The kid, now walking beside the mounted Heckler, was beginning to wonder if there was any real logic in this heavy-footed pilgrimage in the hope of finding the two men each of whom he and his companion hated.

Heckler, however, had found a new impetus and a stiffened spirit in going after Slim Oskin. It flared in him as soon as young Stebbins had mentioned his name. Oskin's doggedness and his gun skill had broken Heckler's reputation and landed him behind bars. For years, he had dreamed of evening up with Oskin. He now saw something like half a chance and was not passing it up and he was powered towards that end by a near insane drive. Somewhere in the region of the creek bed, he might find Oskin and he'd settle with him – provided it could be done with the least danger to himself, probably from ambush. After all, he'd successfully ambushed before, most recently across the creek in the Cherokee Nation.

The kid was now not so sure of what he

had let himself in for. He had been sorely humiliated by Cephas Dannehar on two occasions and his mean disposition craved revenge. But, now that he had dried out, his ire had lessened and he was thinking more logically and thinking that, old-timer Dannehar might be but he was still a sharp-witted and swift gunslinger who, in the gaol at Cinch City, had shown he could think many moves ahead of a raw kid like Stebbins.

Furthermore, Stebbins had doubts about the mental stability of the man he knew as Reese. It seemed increasingly clear that he was plumb vengeance-crazy.

They plodded onward towards the margin of the creek. The sun was bathing the land in strengthening golden light as, one riding and one trudging, they descended a slight hump of thinly wooded land. Below them snaked the silver waters of the creek with a faint trail running along its margin, and on the trail, three riders so close to the pair that they could hear the murmur of their conversation.

'By grab – it's them!' exclaimed Heckler, swinging quickly from the saddle and drawing his Winchester from its scabbard. 'It's them two damned old lawmen and the black guy from Rapid Creek! Right down there under our noses, for the taking.'

Heckler slung the reins of his horse forward to rest across its forelegs to prevent it from wandering and, crouching low, hastened through the cover of the trees. Stebbins, flourishing his borrowed sixgun, came after him, cautiously and with misgivings.

Desperate to seize the moment to loose his Winchester shots at the riders before they were out of his clear view and eager to keep out of sight, Heckler dropped behind the bole of a tree. He wanted Slim Oskin, but his quarry was sided by two companions, a point which Heckler hardly considered in his blood-lust. Then, even as he narrowed his eyes against the glare of the sun, the weight of the opposition dawned on him. He had to hit Oskin with that first shot. Surprise and a speedy follow-up were essential. He pumped a shell into the rifle. At this range and positioned on this high ground, he thought he could bank on firing off three shots and killing the trio below without even calling on the kid's help.

And he would settle with the kid in his own way later. As a bonus, he could add the kid's poke of Dragon wages, lifted from his dead body, to his own getaway funds.

He narrowed his eyes, focused on the skinny rider who was plainly Oskin and squinted along the sights of the weapon.

Down among the three riders, Abel Aubert caught a warning flash of light from among the trees on the rise alongside them – the sun touching the barrel of a weapon. He gave a hoarse shout, dropping his head forward almost into his horse's mane.

'*Duck!*' he bellowed.

Tired though they were, Oskin and Dannehar responded with alertness acquired through their years on the dangerous frontier. Both followed Aubert's example and ducked forward. The Winchester barked and hot lead screeched through the space which Oskin's head had occupied a split second before.

All three swung out of their saddles on the lee side of their animals from the rise with its sniper. Oskin and Aubert cleared leather with their sixguns as they went while Dannehar, swiftly responding to the indications of this being an attack with a rifle, hauled his own Winchester from its scabbard. They squatted on the trail amid the dancing legs of their startled animals.

Up in the trees, Tod Heckler now came near to panic. The moment had been lost, his first shot had failed to hit Oskin and there was no hope of following it with two more to fell his companions. Furthermore, he and the kid were now outnumbered by an alerted enemy who had spotted their place of concealment.

At least he had some advantage in this moment of confusion while the three were on the ground, trying to locate exactly where the shot had come from. He pushed it, partially breaking cover and sending a wild shot down the rise. Somewhere behind him was the kid, armed with his Colt but apparently doing nothing to assist him.

'C'mon, kid, back me up!' roared Heckler.

His wildly aimed bullet *spanged* harmlessly into the dust close to Dannehar.

'It's Heckler – up yonder on the rise! And that kid's with him, close to the trees!' yelled Slim Oskin. The trio rushed forward to run up the rise and Heckler, knowing that his cover was totally blown, came out into the open. He might yet settle all three of them while they were coming up the sloping land, but the detested Oskin was his prime target. He pumped another shell into the Winchester, ducked as a bullet from the pistol of the limping Aubert, running as best he could, screeched close to him. He fired again without careful aim and saw Oskin clap his left hand to his left knee as if hit, but he still continued his run with his gun in hand, closely followed by Dannehar, clutching his rifle. Aubert, hampered by his lame leg, was bringing up the rear.

Heckler was trying to hold down his mounting panic but he was still fired by his hatred of Slim Oskin who, of the three, was drawing closest to him. Where the hell was that kid? he thought and he was gripped by the cold thought that he was in this alone.

Such was the case, for Stebbins, dispirited from the start and realizing that the odds were stacked against Heckler and himself, had had his fill of run-ins with Dannehar and Oskin. He had holstered his borrowed weapon and bolted back into the trees. Heckler's horse was there and he aimed to take it and get well clear of this place.

Heckler was aware that Oskin was close upon him and levelling his Colt again as he ran, half stumbling. Oskin triggered the weapon point-blank at Heckler.

It merely clicked, the striker falling on an empty chamber.

In a horrifying flash, he realized that he had not replenished his sixgun after the fight with the Dragon crew. He was now totally out of ammunition. And Heckler was directly in front of him, somehow having found the courage to stand his ground, pump his Winchester and level it full in Oskin's face. The paunchy gunman was grinning like a wolf. Whatever happened to him in this tight corner, he was going to damned near blow the detested Oskin's head off his shoulders.

A rifle blast roared somewhere close to Oskin's left ear and he saw Tod Heckler go scooting back on his heels, his arms flailing wildly, pitching his rifle into the air. He fell, lifeless as a sack of sand, to the ground.

Oskin turned and saw Cephas Dannehar beside him, smoke dribbling from the mouth of his Winchester.

'I owed you that one for getting me out of that mess when that pair tried to bushwhack me back near the Red River,' said Dannehar calmly.

'Thanks,' breathed Oskin. 'He blamed near had me. I'd used up the rest of my lead in that ruckus back yonder without even realizing it.'

Dannehar made a quick examination of his Winchester as if struck by a sudden thought, then gasped, 'Well, by cracky, I was almost in the same fix. *That shot was the last one in my magazine!'*

Having rested for two days, Dannehar and Oskin were leaving Rapid Creek, with the praises of the Tribal Council and the folk of the settlement ringing in their ears and monetary rewards filling their billfolds. They were in their saddles, riding along the main street. As satisfying to Slim Oskin as anything else was the supply of good, home-cooked grub, packed and forced on them by Abel Aubert's wife.

'I'm not sure we should take money,' muttered Oskin, whose slight knee wound, caused by Heckler's wild shot, had been treated and bandaged. 'We didn't do all that much to earn it.'

'Well, we did a bit,' said Dannehar. 'We're leaving this country knowing the law has been tightened some, and things are in the hands of van Epper and his lawmen, and the Dragon outfit is busted, and Reese or Heckler or whatever he was named is no more, and that smart-alecky kid has taken to his heels and might yet become a responsible citizen and, if that oil stuff really does become important and there is a lake of it under the Cherokee land, they'll benefit from it and not be robbed of it and,

and, and…'

'And what? Go on with the litany if you have any breath left,' said Oskin.

'And I'm bound for Arizona and some extra cash will be useful. I was thinking of heading that way when I was diverted by that letter from Abel Aubert. There's a lady I knew there years ago. I lost out with her but now I hear she's a widow and–'

Oskin halted his mount, cuffed back his hat and blew out his cheeks. 'Well, I'll be roped, branded and hornswoggled!' he declared. 'You never said a word about it in all this time. Not three days ago you were ribbing me about settling down and now it turns out you aim to spark a widow woman. I suppose you want me along as best man.'

Still riding, Dannehar called back. 'I'm merely going to pay my respects to a lady but if a best man should come into the picture, I guess you'll do good as anybody.'

Slim Oskin cuffed his hat further back on his head. 'I'll be hornswoggled!' he repeated. 'I can't believe I'm not being kidded. Still, I'd better come along to keep a restraining hand on you because you'll sure as hell meet some kind of trouble between here and Arizona.'

He spurred his horse forward to join Dannehar where the main street of Rapid Creek became the open trail.

The publishers hope that this book has given you enjoyable reading. Large Print Books are especially designed to be as easy to see and hold as possible. If you wish a complete list of our books please ask at your local library or write directly to:

Dales Large Print Books
Magna House, Long Preston,
Skipton, North Yorkshire.
BD23 4ND